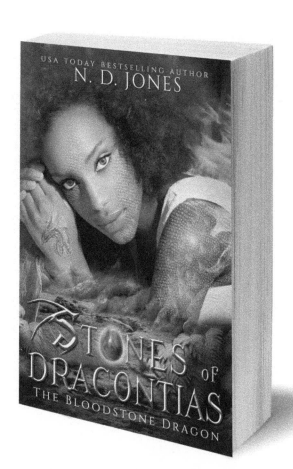

USA TODAY BESTSELLING AUTHOR
N. D. JONES

STONES of
DRACONTIAS
THE BLOODSTONE DRAGON

STONES OF DRACONTIAS
THE BLOODSTONE DRAGON

N.D. Jones

Kuumba
PUBLISHING

Book Layout © 2014 BookDesignTemplates.com
Cover Design by Giusy Ame
Concept Art Design by Phu Thieu
All art and logo copyright © 2017 by Kuumba Publishing

Stones of Dracontias: The Bloodstone Dragon/ N.D. Jones. -- 1st ed.
ISBN: 978-0-9975293-9-5

DEDICATION

This book is dedicated to Helen and Stanley Jenkins. The best in-laws a girl could have.

This is an original character concept art of Kya, the Bloodstone Dragon, and Armstrong Knight.

CHAPTER ONE

Sixty-Seven Years Ago

KYA FLEW BESIDE her oldest sister. Ledisi, a mature green dragon with random specks of gold, contrasted to Kya, a gold dragon who'd inherited her father's coloring over most of her body. Ledisi set a moderate pace, for which the young dragon was grateful. She wasn't yet used to long flights from their island home and to the large populated land of humans. When she'd been a small Dracontias, her four legs good for running around their forest home and not yet capable of flight, she'd flown to places like China, New Zealand and Ethiopia carried in the protective tail of one of her parents.

Now, size and age meant Kya could no longer rely on her parents to ferry her about. Although, with how fatigued she felt a mere two thousand miles from Buto, Kya wouldn't mind taking hold of her sister's tail and allowing Ledisi to tug Kya along in her wake.

She inched closer to her sister, near enough to share the draft of air Ledisi's magic created.

"Tired already, little Bloodstone?" An array of green scales, with a smooth surface and oblong shape arranged in rows along the length of her dorsal, were beautiful in their unmarred perfection. The overlapped

scales fluttered up, a sail opening to the wind currents. Purple wisps of magic drifted from the slots in Ledisi's scales. The drafts of Amethyst magic floated to and under Kya, supporting her Bloodstone magic. *"I will always be there for you, little Bloodstone, even when you grow to maturity and choose a mate."*

Kya had no interest in choosing a mate, and she disliked how all Dracontias now referred to her by the name of the stone in her skull. She'd reached her scale year three months ago, which coincided with the first of these flights with her eldest sister.

For a Dracontias, Kya was still quite young. Years from maturity but no longer a babe in need of watching and coddling. After the Fire of Nyah ritual, her father, ruler of Buto, had anointed her with the title of the Bloodstone Dragon.

Foregoing shame in exchange for a sister's comfort, Kya settled her smaller dragon's body against Ledisi's. Soul Stone Dragon, her sister was known throughout Buto. Her Amethyst healing magic reduced fear and anxiety, protected against psychic attack and promoted trust. She bestowed her purple healing on those worthy of her gift, as was the ancient way of Dracontias.

"In the sky, away from Buto and Father, call me Kya."

"It's an honor to serve as the Bloodstone Dragon. There hasn't been a Dracontias born with the Bloodstone in a thousand years. Your gem is rare and a powerful healing stone."

Supported by Ledisi's magic, the sisters cut through the air at an amazing quickness, now that her sister wasn't moderating her speed to accommodate Kya.

"Your stone cleanses and purifies the blood." Ledisi's snout, cold to Kya's hot, poked her in the neck, playing. *"Your stone also allows you to restore courage, strength, and creativity to those who've lost their way. Your magic has the wonderful power to renew love and friendship."* Another playful poke. *"Would you rather be the Sunstone Dragon?"*

They approached the East Coast of the United States.

Gasira, Kya's older and only brother, despite his ultraviolet green scales, the tip of his tail the only gold on his body, possessed a reddish-brown Dracontias healing stone. His stone had the dubious power of increasing one's sexual energy. Older human males, invariably, prayed to the Sunstone Dragon to help them increase their vitality.

Kya and Ledisi glided to a halt miles above the country's capital.

Her brother's Sunstone helped to alleviate stress and fears. It also had the power to promote independence in the recipient of his healing magic. Despite the other properties of his Dracontias stone, Ledisi, Kya and the rest of the family took much pleasure in teasing Gasira.

"This is where we part."

Kya knew, but she didn't enjoy the thought. Ledisi would continue north to Canada, while she was expected to land, transform and then find a human who could broaden her understanding of them.

"Perhaps, this once, you'll permit me to travel with you."

Before she'd completed her sentence, Ledisi's tail had snapped out and pushed against Kya's side. Not hard and malicious but with enough force to remind the young dragon of her responsibility.

"The Fire of Nyah ritual," Ledisi began, *"reminds us of our intention and purpose in life. We possess healing stones for a reason, Bloodstone Dragon. But how can we, who claim the sky and the ground, understand humans and their nature if we have never lived their experiences?"*

"We know their nature. They're violent and selfish. They pray without thought. They offer only to receive. And they understand us even less than Father thinks we understand them."

Kya would never utter such words of opposition in front of her parents. With Ledisi, however, there was no emotion or thought she couldn't share freely with her eldest sister.

"Not all humans are as you describe. Don't judge the many by the actions of the few. We heal the worthy. We cast off our hard dragon scales in exchange for soft human flesh to remind ourselves of the fragility of life."

Ledisi sounded too much like their father. Of her siblings, only Gasira shared her skepticism of humans.

"Father is a wise dragon." Ledisi reached out to Kya with her soothing magic. *"He doesn't trust blindly. Our ability to transform is a secret no one beyond our island home is aware. Now that you're of age, you must shift and learn how to walk among humans, your mind no longer in the clouds."*

"I much prefer the safety of the sky than the dangers found on the ground of humans."

Kya lowered her eyes to the bustling city below. Hundreds of feet in the air, she could see them, specks of entitlement and short lifespans. They were loud, smelled, and polluted the oceans from which she drank and the air she marveled in flying through.

"Meet me here in a week. Father will expect a report, and I don't wish to lie to him again. You must shift this time. Find a human worthy of your trust and make a friend. Maybe you'll find a diata in this City of Magnificent Intentions."

A human as brave as a dragon? She doubted that but argued no more with her sister. Ledisi had indulged Kya's bout of ideological rebellion, she wouldn't repay her patience with obstinacy.

Kya watched her sister fly away, stunning green scales twinkling in the midday sun.

She flew toward Washington, D.C. The smell of garbage and sweat worsened the closer she drew to the ground. Landing with a soft thud, Kya glanced around. An alley, dirty and empty. She supposed it was a perfect location for her change. Private, if not sanitary. She could conjure human clothing after her transformation, although she didn't relish the idea of confining her dragon's soul in such a tiny form.

Despite the sun high in the sky, the alley held little light. A ten-foot locked metal fence lay at one end of the alley, behind Kya. The other end led to the street, where she could hear everything from disgruntled workers in the building across the street to rats scurrying in the sewers below.

She should shift now, but something kept her from doing so. Instead, she settled behind a dumpster, her four legs tucked under her, her snout to the disgusting ground. Kya would rest for a few minutes, shift and then go in search of a creature more mythical than dragons—an honorable human.

"Please, let me go."

Kya awoke at the soft, desperate plea. She hadn't meant to fall asleep. The sun, once warm and bright, had given way to a crescent moon.

"Please, please, let me go."

A woman. Young.

"Now why would we do something like that?"

A man's voice, deep and confident. He smelled of alcohol. Lots of it.

"You're so pretty. We like pretty, sweet things. Don't we, Ron?"

"Yeah, yeah, we do."

Two males and one crying female.

Kya heard clothes rip and more crying. She didn't understand the context of the human interaction. What she did comprehend, however, was the woman's fear. The singular scent, above all the others, had Kya's scales rising and anger flaring.

"Hold her down for me. Yeah, Ronny boy, just like that." The man's voice lowered, but Kya could still hear every cruel word. "Don't fight, girlie, or Ron here will cut that pretty face of yours. Just stay still. I promise, you'll enjoy it."

Kya may have been a dragon and spent little time around humans, but she wasn't naïve to what transpired between males and females regardless of the species. She didn't know the human word for what the men wanted to do the female, and it didn't matter.

Her whimpers and frightened pleas did.

She stood, silent and lethal.

Two men, one woman indeed. All three on the ground. Her hands were held over her head, trapped at the wrist by one of the men. The other man knelt between her spread legs, his knees holding them opened and his fingers working to push his pants below his waist.

Kya would kill him first. She'd never had a taste for human blood and flesh. Today, though, she'd make an exception.

The door from the building to her left slammed open. Kya watched as a man burst from the bar and into the alley.

"I knew it, you pieces of shit."

The enraged man flung himself at the man who hovered over the woman, kicking him in the face and sending the shocked man backward.

"What in the—"

Fists connected with the male still holding the woman down. Kya heard breaking, probably the man's nose, which bled blood fire down his face.

"You think you can come to this neighborhood and hurt our women?"

More punches, vicious blows which had the bleeding man falling onto his back, hands and arms doing little to ward off the bigger man's attack.

From her spot near the dumpster, Kya did nothing as the man, the diata, dismantled the two men, thrashing them with his hands, feet and words. Clutching her ripped shirt with trembling hands, the human female ran through the open door. A minute later, she returned with three men.

"All right, Knight. We got this, man. Jesus, the Secret Service won't accept your application if you get arrested." He pushed the woman's savior toward the mouth of the alley. "Go, we got this. You don't need to be here when the cops arrive."

The man, Knight, pulled his shirt over his head and handed it to the woman. The blood of the men, writhing on the alley floor, speckled the sleeve of the garment. The woman didn't seem to care, for she tugged it on without haste.

"Go," the man said again, his finger gesturing in the direction of the street.

Knight went, his boots hitting the pavement as he ran, back bare and glistening with sweat.

To her surprise, Kya not only found herself not minding the human's sweaty scent but taking to the sky in noiseless pursuit of the diata.

———◦◦———

Armstrong grimaced when the hot water from the shower hit his cut and bleeding knuckles. He'd have to ice his fists before he turned in for the night. Closing his eyes and shifting fully under the spray of water, Armstrong fought to regulate his breathing and calm his anger.

When he'd seen those men tonight, first one and then the other, approach the young woman who sat at a corner table, he knew they were up to no good. Sure, the girl, maybe nineteen, if a day, shouldn't have been in the bar in that part of DC and by herself. Far too pretty and innocent for the local flavor, the girl stood out the minute she stepped into the joint.

Armstrong didn't know if she'd been given bad directions, someone was playing a joke on her, or whether she was one of those females who got off on living dangerously and testing boundaries. He hadn't known her story, and he hadn't cared. From his perch at the bar, he'd seen her reject, with a definitive shake of her head, the tall blond guy with a bad haircut and even worse taste in clothing. She'd given his friend, who'd approached a few minutes after the first, the same rigorous head shake.

The men had left the girl alone after that, or so Armstrong had thought. In the men's room, he'd overheard the assholes and hadn't liked a damn thing they'd said. So, he'd watched them watch her for over an hour.

The soap stung his bruised fists. They throbbed, but it was a good kind of pain. The kind that came with the satisfaction of being in the right place at the right time and doing the right thing. Hell, he knew, this close to his interview with the US Secret Service, he didn't need to do anything stupid that would ruin his chances. He'd been keeping his nose clean for the last six months. No fights. Hardly any drinking. And damn near no women. He liked all three too much, according to his brother Isaiah, the owner of Knight Life Bar.

Isaiah had been right when he'd told Armstrong to disappear. The cops would have a lot of questions. His older brother, a smooth talker from way back, could handle DCPD. The man could talk his way out of damn near anything, which had saved their asses over the years. Isaiah had kept them in school, off the streets, and out of jail when too many neighborhood guys had taken the wrong path to manhood. The cradle to prison pipeline in his neighborhood was all too real.

He toweled off. Armstrong contemplated shaving, then decided against it. The bathroom mirror, thanks to his broken exhaust, had steamed over and the bathroom was too muggy for anything more than a quick brush of the teeth. Two minutes later, he strolled buck naked across the cool wood of his living room floor and into his kitchen. Snatching the black kitchen towel from the oven door handle, Armstrong opened the freezer and shoveled a handful of ice into the towel.

It was a little after one in the morning, maybe he'd catch an old western on television while he iced down his knuckles. Either the action would keep him awake long enough to do both hands or the corny dialogue would put him to sleep.

He grabbed a can of soda from the frig, turned off the kitchen light, and made his way to the living room.

He stopped. Blinked. Rubbed his eyes. Blinked again.

What in the hell?

Grape can of soda, ice, and towel were dropped from his hands. Armstrong was also sure his mouth hung open. He couldn't feel his fingers or toes. And his brain, something was wrong with his brain because all he could think about was he stood in front of a dragon buck naked.

Not that there was an actual dragon in his home, one who'd entered his apartment and he hadn't heard a thing. Not that a hungry-looking dragon stared at Armstrong from a crouched position beside his couch. No, none of that registered with him. Instead, his stupid brain thought about post-shower shrinkage and first impressions.

More out of embarrassment than modesty, Armstrong covered himself with all he had. His hands.

The dragon didn't move. It only watched him. He didn't know what to do. Armstrong figured if the creature had intended to eat or kill him, it would've gobbled him up already. That was his human brain rationalizing an absurd situation. He had no idea how dragons thought. They were majestic beasts he'd admired his entire life.

The world knew little about them, except they always seemed to be part of human history. Where dinosaurs had died out, leaving behind fossils to mark their time there, the dragons remained.

They flew, healed, and disappeared. No one knew where they went when they weren't answering the prayers of humans or flying away from cameras.

From the little he could see of the dragon, with no light on in the living room, Armstrong could hazard a guess as to which dragon had invaded his home with its scaly presence. The youngest dragon among the ones humans had cataloged over the years. Until tonight, he'd never seen it alone. Normally, the dragon flew beside much larger dragons. Its family, he assumed. Not that there was anything small about the reptile.

Why haven't you screamed or run away in terror?

"Did you just speak in my mind?" He shook his head, then smacked his forehead. Twice.

That's quite unnecessary. Your brain's function is at it should be. Otherwise, I wouldn't be able to communicate with you telepathically.

"This isn't happening. Dragons aren't telepaths." He glanced around his apartment. No broken glass. How in the hell had the dragon gotten in there? "I'm dreaming. That must be it."

I thought you would be more intelligent than this. Thus far, you've proven to be quite a disappointment. And why are you not screaming? Do I not frighten you?

Without thinking, Armstrong lowered his hands and took three steps into the living room. "Are you the cute gold dragon I've seen on TV?"

A huge head rose, the crown skimming the ceiling. Two rows of sharp, white teeth glistened, forked tongue hissed and eyes dilated.

I am the Bloodstone Dragon, and you will show me the proper respect. Dragons are not cute, Knight.

"How do you know my name?"

Why have you not run? Do you possess no sense of self-preservation?

"Do you want me to be afraid of you? Did you come here to scare me?"

You're a strange human. I don't pretend to understand why you don't react the way a normal human would.

"If I did, we wouldn't be having this nice conversation. To answer your question, I'm not afraid of you. You're big and have those scary ass teeth, and I should've beat feet to get the hell out of here." He shrugged. "I don't know how to explain it, but I know you won't hurt me."

The dragon lowered its head again, settling its face on the floor, its tail curled around what looked to be back legs.

Armstrong smiled and moved three steps closer. The dragon was trying to not break the cheap furniture he had in his home by making itself as small as possible. He wondered how long the dragon had been there, waiting for him to notice its presence and run away screaming.

"Are you male or female, Bloodstone Dragon?"

For the first time, serpent eyes took in the most obvious symbol of his gender. If the dragon had been a woman, gazing at him the way it was, he would cover himself again because the dragon didn't seem impressed.

Female, like the human you saved in the alley.

"Wait, you were there? I didn't see you."

You also didn't see me until I made myself known. You aren't very observant.

He was plenty observant, that's how he'd known what the two ass-holes had in mind. A sexy woman had come up to him, asking Armstrong to buy her a drink. Five minutes of flirting were all it had taken for him to lose track of the men and their quarry. A few minutes more and the men would've raped the girl. Luckily, his big head had stepped in and reminded his little head that he was supposed to be keeping an eye on the young woman.

Returning to the mess he'd made on the floor, Armstrong retrieved the soda and scooped up the ice and hand towel. Dragon or not, he was thirsty and still needed to ice down his bruised knuckles. If she'd seen the fight, then she would understand.

He plopped onto the couch, the dragon's head, even lowered, came nearly to the armrest.

The men wanted to hurt the female. I could smell her fear and their lust. The scent of both lingers, as does the sound of your fists beating them into bloody submission. I didn't think I would find a diata. I'm glad I did.

"Diata? What does that mean?"

Brave as a dragon. You even roared when you saw the first man.

"Did I?"

He hadn't known. Armstrong had seen only red when he'd come through the side door of the bar. The one guy was right there, so close to violating the girl that all he wanted to do was knock his goddamn teeth down his throat. He'd settled for introducing his heavy work boot to the man's drunk face.

Yes, you sounded quite feral. Like a baby dragon. Diata indeed.

"Why are you here?"

My sister told me to find a human friend. Instead, I found a diata.

The dragon's voice had a soothing effect, the longer she spoke in his mind. The few aches from the fight ebbed, and his fists no longer hurt.

They tingled, but nothing more than that wispy sensation. Armstrong thought he saw red vapors rise from where the dragon laid on his floor.

"Is this a dream?"

No, Knight. I'm real. The next time I visit, however, I will seek permission before entering your home.

Armstrong was so tired, he could hardly keep his eyes open.

Sleep, diata, and let my magic take care of your wounds.

"Armstrong Knight. That's my name. But I like the way diata sounds in my mind. You have a very nice voice, Bloodstone Dragon."

He swore she laughed in his mind.

You've never known the touch of a dragon's magic. I should've taken that into consideration before I used my healing powers. The first few times tend to produce a drugging effect, especially the first.

Heavy eyelids fluttered shut, grape soda and melting ice forgotten. But not the dragon. He could hear nothing, but Armstrong knew she was still there.

"What's your name?"

I told you. I'm the Bloodstone Dragon.

"That's a title. What's your real name? Do dragons have real names?"

She didn't answer, but she did shift on the floor.

With effort, Armstrong forced his eyes to part. She was gone. With a bolt, he sat up. Armstrong wanted to leap from the couch, run to the window and see where the dragon had gone. Instead, the magic that floated around Armstrong urged him into restful compliance.

Pulling his legs onto the couch, he reclined, feeling safe, courageous and strong. For the first time since deciding to apply for the Secret Service, Armstrong Knight didn't fear the federal agency would pass over a black man because of his race. If they did, it would be their loss, not his.

He fell asleep, certain he'd heard a voice in his head say, *Kya.*

CHAPTER TWO

WHY KYA CHOSE this human, she didn't know. Armstrong Knight wasn't at all what she'd expected. In the alley, when he'd defended the woman, outraged on her behalf, she thought him diata. Yet later, in his dwelling, the man didn't have the good sense to flee when he found an apex predator in his home. Not that dragons preyed on humans, but that fact missed the point. A weaker creature should know when to tread with caution while in the presence of a superior being.

Did his human parents not warn him of the dangers of speaking to strangers? Kya had once heard a human mother scold her small child for doing the same thing Knight had done last night. He should've sought safety by running away. The fact he had not, choosing to converse with her, had served to remind Kya the naked man was still the diata she'd seen earlier.

Brave, even in the face of a dragon. Her father would think the human demented, which he may still prove to be. Yet Kya, as she approached the roof of Knight's building, didn't know what to make of the man.

Arms waving in the air, he whistled and jumped up and down. Did the human think her hearing and vision impaired? Why was he shining a light? Dragons could see fine in the dark.

Monitoring her rate of descent, Kya took extra care to not land too hard and displace Knight from the roof. Her father wouldn't be pleased if she killed a human, even if accidentally. Her back legs reached the ground first, sturdy and wide. Claws and weight crushed a layer of gravel, but it held her, so she touched her front legs to the roof and let it bear the full of Kya's weight.

The light she'd seen moments ago swung back and forth, moving from one part of her body to the next.

"Jesus, you're gold all over. I mean, gold, gold." The light flashed brightly in her eyes, and Kya hissed at the man. "Ah, sorry. I didn't get a good look at you last night. I knew you were the cute gold dragon, but I had no idea how gold you really are. Not a yellow-orange gold but metallic gold. Beautiful. May I touch you?" Knight reached out his hand to do just that, but another hiss from Kya had him yanking his hand back. "Okay. Too soon for touching. Got it."

Again, Kya wondered why this human wasn't afraid of her. She also questioned why she found herself thinking about him these past two days when she was supposed to hunt for a worthy human from which she could learn. Despite Ledisi's directive, she hadn't yet shifted and walked among the humans. Well, except for that first night. She'd had to shift to enter Knight's dwelling. Magic had done the rest, unlocking his front door and letting her inside.

He could never know her secret, so she'd found the only location in his home that could accommodate a creature of her size. The fit, while tight, was large enough for her to manage if she didn't move her tail or head too much.

Knight walked away from Kya and to a silver foldable chair. He sat, pulled out a can from a bag beside his chair, opened it and drank.

"Grape soda. I would offer you a can, but I guess dragons don't drink stuff like this." When he finished his drink, he crushed the empty can between his hands and then tossed it into the same brown paper bag. "When I woke up, the other day, I thought I dreamed it all." He raised the back of his hands to Kya. "Until I saw these. Healed and perfect. I know I didn't dream that fight or my bruised knuckles. Thank you, by the way. I would've been okay healing the old-fashioned way, but I appreciate your kindness."

He appreciated her kindness? His sincere words had Kya stepping closer, head low as to not tower over the human more than she already was. Then again, his lack of fear was clear as was Knight's interest in seeing all of her.

Kya lifted her head high, the way dragons were supposed to present themselves and stopped mere feet in front of him. Apparently, the non-verbal invitation was all the man required.

Knight jumped from his chair, his light back in his hand and on.

"Thank you. I know it's rude to gawk, but this is an opportunity of a lifetime. And, umm, it's only fair. You saw me naked."

I didn't ask to see you in a state of undress.

"True, but you get what you get when you enter a man's apartment with no notice."

Fair enough, Knight. Gaze until you grow tired of looking at the same color.

Squatting, he shined the light on her tail and then onto her back legs.

"You got some green mixed in. Stomach, feet, tail. Faint but there."

While dragons ranged in color from gold to green, her father, the Aragonite Star Dragon, was the only true gold dragon. Even Kya, who most resembled her father of all his offspring, had also inherited the green of her mother's scales, the same color of ferns that grew on Buto.

"I'm glad you returned." Knight pushed to his feet, so tiny in comparison to Kya. "It's strange. I wanted to call you." He laughed. "Dragons don't use telephones. I was working when I heard you in my head again. I almost fell off the scaffold." Another laugh, tinged with nervousness. "I work construction. I'm not afraid of heights, so I'm always on the top platform."

After taking in his fill of Kya, while speaking of things she didn't understand, Knight returned to his chair and sat.

"You're quiet tonight."

You speak enough for the both of us.

"The Knights have the gift of gab, Kya."

She'd forgotten she'd told him her name. Against the rules. Kya would have to be more cautious when dealing with humans, particularly this human who, despite his gregarious nature and lack of self-preservation, possessed a keen mind.

"That's a nice name. You can call me Armstrong. Knight seems a little formal after you've seen a man naked." He found another can in his paper bag, opened it and sipped. "Or diata. I like that, too."

Kya bent her knees and settled her long body on the gravel. Armstrong enjoyed the sound of his voice. Kya needed to learn more about humans. Why not from this strange but kind man?

I need a guide, Armstrong, in the ways of human thought and behavior. Will you be my guide?

"A cross-cultural exchange, you mean?" He appeared interested, his elbows on his knees and back leaned forward.

Not an exchange. I cannot share dragon life with outsiders.

"That's pretty one-sided."

True. But it's how we've survived and will continue to survive. I will, however, grant you one wish and two questions in exchange for your service as my human guide.

The man's teeth were quite white when he smiled at her. She'd chosen well, this Armstrong Knight of Washington, DC. He possessed a dragon's soul and a protective heart. The human wouldn't take advantage of the unorthodox offer she'd made him. Dragons didn't grant wishes beyond that of their healing stone magic.

"Two questions and a wish?"

Yes.

"Must I do all three tonight?"

You do not. But it's only fair I offer a token of goodwill tonight if you agree to the exchange.

"You've already given me a token of goodwill. You're not only here, but you've permitted me to look you over with my flashlight. If you were a human female and I stared at you like I did, I would've been slapped. Dragons heal and leave. Until two days ago, I had no idea dragons spoke at all. So you see, Kya, there's already been a cross-cultural exchange between us."

Which was why she was supposed to learn from humans by pretending to be one of them. She upbraided herself for not taking her father's teachings to heart and practice. Kya needed to listen more and question less. Was it too late to begin anew with Armstrong as a human female?

Kya had no skill in pretending to be what she wasn't. The physical shift was easy enough to make but being a human entailed more than looking like one. She was out of her depth and didn't feel confident she could convince a man as smart as Armstrong to befriend and trust an unusual human woman.

Her strength was in being a dragon, but an ignorant dragon in the body of a human would yield little. Besides, Kya rather liked the way Armstrong looked upon her natural form. Not with fear but with curiosity and respect. He saw her, Kya, and she wasn't ashamed to admit she enjoyed the human's interest.

"If I asked your age, would that count as one of my questions?"

Why does my age matter?

"It doesn't. I'm twenty-five. My birthday is March twenty-ninth. I have an older brother, Isaiah, and two younger sisters, Clarice and Janet. My father died when I was thirteen. It was hard not having him around, but Isaiah stepped in and stepped up."

Kya didn't know how to respond to anything Armstrong had shared, especially about the death of his father. He'd stated that fact of his life with the same flat voice as he uttered the others. Yet, his scent betrayed his calm exterior.

Sadness. Grief.

Kya had never known either emotion. Dragons were long-lived, although not immortal. They grew old and died. Nothing could kill them as far as she knew. Unlike humans, they didn't get sick, not even what humans called the "common cold."

I'm the youngest dragon.

"In your family?"

I'm the youngest dragon of all dragons. We don't age as humans do.

She thought, trying to calculate her age in terms of human years. If she told him her hatch year, she didn't think her response would adequately answer his question. She grasped the underlining meaning of his query. What he wanted to know was her age in relation to his own.

He'd seen her with her parents and siblings, smaller and weaker, and he'd assumed, correctly, she was younger than the others. What he didn't know was how much younger.

What is the age when a human is considered a young adult?

"Eighteen. We can vote at that age but not drink."

Then I'm eighteen.

"You're so young. My mother would call you a baby, although I'm sure you were born before her."

When Father isn't around, Mother permits me to tuck my head in her neck and breathe in her scent. I'm too old for such cossetting, I know, but I cherish those moments more than I should.

"Siblings?"

One brother and six sisters.

With each shared fact of family and home, Armstrong moved closer to Kya until he laid on his back in front of her nose. He smelled of a spice scent but no fear for how close he was to a dragon's mouth and fangs. The human really was quite unusual.

"If I touch you, will you run away like you did when I asked you your name?"

Dragons do not run away. It was simply time for my departure.

"Yeah, riiiight, whatever you say, Bloodstone Dragon."

Mock me at your peril, Armstrong Knight. Is that your one wish, to touch a dragon?

He shook his head. "Without trying, I can name five hospitals with centers dedicated to children with cancer. Do you know what cancer is?"

I do, but knowledge of diseases that afflict humans isn't necessary for dragons to heal them. If the human is worthy of our gift, we grant it freely. Is that your wish?

"Yeah, is it too much to ask?"

How many children?

"I don't know. I don't expect you to heal every kid with cancer. I don't even know how long that would take or how long you'll be here. But some kids are worse off than others and will die if something can't be done to help them. Trust me, Kya, very little can be done to help them. Children would be worthy of your healing magic, I would think."

You want nothing for yourself?

"I just asked for something for me. For however long you're here, will you heal as many children with cancer as you can? That's my wish."

A strange human indeed. Kya was prepared to grant Armstrong most anything, although she'd imagined his request would reflect what she'd come to think of as the shallow and selfish nature of a human's heart. Perhaps Ledisi was correct. Kya shouldn't judge the many by the actions of the few.

After tonight, she had less than four days before her sister would return for her and they'd fly home to Buto. Armstrong's wish, while admirable, would challenge Kya. She'd never healed a human without the watchful eye and guiding magic of one of her parents or a sibling. What she'd done for Armstrong, two nights ago, was her first independent act of healing.

His injuries weren't severe, and not life-threatening like cancer. The greater the damage to the human, physical or psychological, the more magic and skill required of the dragon. His wish would take time.

I will do my best, diata.

He shifted onto his side, so very close to her nose. But he didn't reach for her despite the way his hand twitched on the graveled ground between them.

"I know you will. You would've killed those men in the alley if I hadn't gotten to them first, wouldn't you?"

Yes, I was prepared to do so. The thought of eating such vile creatures was sickening. But I couldn't do nothing while they hurt the woman further.

"You really are young. Seeing you would've sent the bastards running and saved the girl. You wouldn't have needed to upset your stomach by eating those maggots."

You didn't run away from me.

"I'm not them. May I touch you? Your gold scales call to me. I don't know why."

To her discomfort and confusion, Kya desired the human's touch. She scooted away from the hand raised above her nose before lifting inches into the air. If Armstrong was intent on touching her, she'd left herself within his reach. But he wouldn't because he was an honorable man, and she hadn't granted him permission to lay hands upon her.

My scales are too sharp for your tender human flesh. Dragon scales may resemble the snakes you're used to, but ours are not harmless to the touch.

Disappointment bloomed across his face before he hid it behind a smile. Armstrong lowered his hand, and Kya felt a stab of guilt. She neither enjoyed the sensation nor appreciated the emotions this human created within her.

I can, however, use magic to soften my scales so you won't sever your hand if you insist on petting me as if I'm a domesticated animal.

A loud bark of laughter. "You, a domesticated animal? I don't think so. First, you could barely fit in my living room. Second, I would never insult you by thinking of or treating the Bloodstone Dragon as I would a dog or cat. I don't want to pet you, Kya, I want to touch you, know you. That's not the same."

It wasn't the same. It was worse.

Kya concentrated, her attention inward and on the magic that was her birthright. She saw her skin and the scales that grew from it. Thick,

STONES OF DRACONTIAS: THE BLOODSTONE DRAGON · 21

heavy, and sharp for protection. Scales were a dragon's last line of defense. She learned at an early age how to adjust the strength of them, a natural shield for her kind.

The adjustments, however, normally increased not decreased, although that direction was also within her power. As she shifted the texture and density of her scales, the magic and focus required much the same as when she shifted into her human form. Kya breathed magic through the vents of her scales.

She envisioned a malleable human bed, capable of comfort and support. The change tingled, the way it did when Kya cast her magic with purpose and heart.

Touch me where you will, Armstrong, my scales welcome your hand.

At his boyish smile, Kya returned to the rooftop. She reclined, as she'd done before.

She didn't know what she expected from the human, but it wasn't the feel of his face against hers. Kya had assumed Armstrong would explore her tail, maybe her wide flank or even the nose he'd been so close to minutes earlier. Instead, he leaned in and pressed his cheek below her right eye. Hands came up and rested beside his head, palms against her and so very small and warm.

"This is our first hug of what I hope will be many. Thank you. I appreciate your trust. I'll never betray anything you tell or show me. We Knights aren't built for betrayal."

Neither were dragons.

CHAPTER THREE

KYA WAS EXHAUSTED, and she still had thousands of miles to go before she reached Buto. After the last four days, she couldn't wait to see the green of her island home and bask in the fresh air. There was a stench to sickness, Kya had known, but the aroma of dying children was unlike anything she'd smelled before or hoped to smell again.

Yet she would because there was nothing like curing a dying child and seeing the child healthy and running about pounds lighter for the pain lifted from shoulders too small to carry its weight. Parents had cried and thanked Kya. Doctors marveled and gazed upon her with gratitude. Nurses had invited her back, although from the questioning looks on their faces they were unsure if she comprehended their language.

She did. But Kya wouldn't make the same mistake twice. She'd remained silent, flying away before they could take too many pictures of her. To Kya's annoyance and dismay, Armstrong's wish meant she'd had little time to visit the human on the roof of his apartment building. She was annoyed she'd missed him and dismayed she had to leave without saying goodbye in person.

Kya had flown past the building where he told her he worked, hoping to spot him on the scaffold. It rained then, as it did now, so there were no humans outside on what looked to be an unsafe structure.

I must return home, diata.

She spoke in his mind. He would hear her. Kya's telepathy extended thousands of miles. Once she approached the protective mists of Buto, however, her telepathic link to the human would be severed.

I look forward to seeing and speaking with you again. Be safe, Armstrong Knight. And have faith. Your dreams are well within your reach.

Kya had enjoyed Armstrong's company more than she ought. More than she would reveal to him or even to Ledisi, who flew toward her.

Fast.

Why was she moving so fast? A second later, Kya's question was answered in the form of an armored helicopter. Kya had seen planes in the air before, but nothing like the one that chased her sister.

Gray like the rainy sky, the helicopter's blades whirled through the air. Men in green-and-black uniforms pointed weapons from the open door. One of the weapons fired. A large net shot from it and toward her sister.

Ledisi slashed through the sky, cutting to the right and avoiding the net. Instead of continuing her path toward Kya, Ledisi banked left and the helicopter followed.

More nets were cast out, and Ledisi avoided each one. She didn't attack the humans pursuing her, even when bullets rang out.

Kya roared. How dare the humans attempt to harm the Soul Stone Dragon.

She flew in the direction her sister had gone.

"No, Kya, stay away. I can handle this."

"But they're trying to hurt you."

"Their bullets cannot penetrate my armor. But they may be capable of slicing through your young scales. Make them as strong as possible, Bloodstone Dragon, and keep your distance."

Kya rarely disobeyed. Yet the urge to do so had fire churning in her belly with the force to hunt, protect, and kill.

What would she do if Ledisi didn't return? What would Kya tell her parents if she returned home without their eldest offspring? Unlike other species, dragons didn't give birth but once every two to three hundred years. It had taken four hundred years between her mother's last hatchling for Kya to be born. By dragon standards, her parents were quite old, which also meant they were powerful beyond reckoning.

These humans did not want to begin a war with the Dracontias.

In the distance, she heard the Soul Stone Dragon roar. Ledisi was a full-grown and experienced dragon, she reminded herself. Her scales were tough and her magic even stronger.

Still, the absence of her sister by her side frightened Kya. Even more so than the second helicopter she heard coming toward her.

It approached fast, but not as fast as Kya could fly.

She took off. Kya knew not to fly in the direction Ledisi had gone or toward Buto.

The helicopter pursued, and she flew faster. Magic curled around Kya and propelled her through the sky. The same nets Ledisi had so easily avoided, Kya was fairing less impressively.

She'd never flown defensively or with a rush of anger and fear that had her throat burning.

Not just burning, but hot from pain. She'd been shot. More than once. The bullets hadn't gone in, but the impact hurt. Kya tried to focus on strengthening her scales, but the high-speed chase and barrage of bullets made it difficult to recall her training.

She dipped, slowed, and let the helicopter fly over her. Pivoting, Kya flew in the opposite direction. She couldn't maintain her rate of speed, not after having spent four days flying all over the United States and using her healing magic at over a dozen cancer centers.

Kya felt her magic and strength wane. She tried to fight through the fatigue. Tried to stay ahead of the helicopter that had turned and was once again hunting her with determination.

When the net came this time, Kya was too slow. The tight net fell over her head and half of her body. Clawing with her front legs, she tore at the net, which was stronger than she thought. But not strong enough to contain the Bloodstone Dragon.

It ripped, and Kya breathed easier.

Another net caught her. Then another. And another still, until her head and legs were tangled.

Losing her equilibrium, Kya plummeted. She struggled against the webbing, using teeth and claws. These nets felt wrong, strong in a way that suggested they were made to do exactly this.

Capture a dragon. A small dragon. The first helicopter hadn't been after Ledisi. It had served as a diversion, a well-planned distraction to draw the older, bigger and stronger Soul Stone Dragon away from the easier prey.

Kya.

Opening her mouth as far as she could, Kya blasted the nets with her fire magic, singeing them but not much more. She breathed deeply, fought her fear of crashing into the Pacific Ocean from such a high altitude, and blew a continuous stream of fire.

Too close. Dragon fire wasn't meant to be released so close to the originating dragon. But Kya had no choice, so she closed her eyes and pushed even more fire from her swiftly falling body.

She crashed into the ocean. The burning nets coiled about her frame. Kya couldn't get free. The more she struggled, the more the nets twisted around her sinking frame. Down she went, deeper under the water.

No air.

Two helicopters joined her in the ocean, a great tidal wave of a crash. Metal burned, men screamed, and Kya continued her breathless descent.

She was going to drown.

"Kya? Kya?"

From a distance and between the slowing pulse of her heartbeats, Kya heard her sister in her head. Ledisi had come for her.

Tired. Kya was so tired, and the net around her neck made breathing so very difficult.

"Kya?"

The ocean wanted her, and she had no strength to object.

Down.

Down.

———◦———

"What's got you down in the dumps?"

Armstrong sipped from the beer he'd been nursing for the better part of an hour as Isaiah wiped down the bar. Scratched from age and wear, the thick wood was still a beauty. It had, like the Knight family, withstood much.

"You got the job you wanted, which Mom is still bragging about to her church friends. Two months later, and I still can't go into the house with you by my side without her pushing me out of the way to get to you." Isaiah chuckled. "Maybe some of that momma love will swing back to me when I give Mom her first grandbaby."

"Wait, is Nicole pregnant?"

"Not yet. We're working on it."

"Working on it? It's called having sex with your beautiful wife. Dad gave you the talk before he died, so I know you know where everything goes."

Isaiah threw the wet, lemon-scented washrag at Armstrong, who caught it before the nasty thing hit him in the face.

"Like I said, we're working on it. When you're married, you gotta fit sex in when you can. We're both busy and work different hours."

"That defeats the whole point of getting married. Sex after marriage shouldn't be complicated. She's there. You're there. Sex should happen."

"Says the single man who hasn't had sex in how long, Armstrong?"

"By choice."

"Whatever. Is your mood about a woman?"

"Not exactly. I met someone. I thought she liked me, but I haven't seen her in weeks."

"So call her. Better yet, get off your moping ass and go see the woman."

He wished he could call or go see Kya. Armstrong didn't regret his wish, but it had kept the dragon from visiting him on the rooftop again. Arrogant the Bloodstone Dragon may be, Kya was also sarcastic, intelligent and fun to talk to. If she were a human woman, Armstrong would put a ring on her finger so fast it would make both their heads spin.

She wasn't, so the thought was pointless and stupid. But they were friends, or so Armstrong had thought. Since her last message in his head, however, she hadn't contacted him. A part of Armstrong worried something awful may have happened to her. Despite being a dragon, Kya was also young and naïve. He didn't doubt she was at least a hundred years older than Armstrong. Which, as she'd told him, human time and dragon development weren't the same. For all intents and purposes, Kya was the same age as the girl in the alley.

No wonder she was going to have the men for a late-night snack.

Then there was the insecure side of him who thought their talk on the rooftop had meant more to Armstrong than it did to Kya. That once she returned home, she looked back on their few hours together as a short footnote in her long life. Armstrong Knight, a novelty for the young dragon and nothing more.

"Where did you go?"

Armstrong downed the dregs of his beer. "I'm right here, and I can't call or go see her. I don't have her number or know where she lives. Besides, it's not like that between us. Kya's my friend."

"Yeah, whatever. Whenever you decide to pull your head from your ass, I'd like to meet your friend Kya."

Belatedly, Armstrong glanced around the bar. At four in the afternoon, few people were there and only him at the bar. Dammit, he should've kept his big fat mouth shut about Kya, even to Isaiah. If she returned, and he prayed she did, he would have to do a better job of keeping her and their friendship a secret.

The Circle of Drayke, ten men of power, wealth and influence, sat around a large conference table. *Big Ben's* quarter bells chimed in the background as they watched the grainy black-and-white footage on the screen. Captain Rudolph stood in the rear of the room, ignored by the robber barons who thought themselves captains of industry and a friend to the common man. They wielded their money like a sword, their sterling reputation their shield.

They came from around the world, a meeting of men of means no one would question. They lived lavished lifestyles and bought what they wanted. That included people. People like Captain Winston Rudolph and the soldiers under his command. Growing up in Gary, West Virginia, the son of a coal miner, Rudolph knew he had two choices, the mine or the military.

He'd chosen the military and never looked back. Years later, who would've thought the skinny kid from Gary, who went to bed hungry many a night, would be rubbing elbows with men born with silver spoons in their mouths.

He despised each of them. Their arrogance and intolerance. But mostly their discontent. How could men who had so much want even more? What they wanted was crazy. Even their name, ridiculous by a normal person's reasoning, spoke to their hubris. The name Drakye meant to possess the power of a dragon. Bull, but that was the men's desire. Not just knowledge of the creatures or even one to cage and parade about like a tamed circus freak, but the actual magic and strength of a dragon.

Ten men. Ten families. A legacy of researching dragons for whatever made them special. To date, they still didn't know. At this rate, and with the help of mercenaries like him, they soon would.

"Good first attempt with the nets. I'll get my research and design department to make them bigger and stronger." Hugh Cafferty spoke to Rudolph but hadn't the courtesy to turn and face the man. Instead, he sipped from his cognac and watched Rudolph's failed mission to capture the gold dragon. "It's small, probably still a baby by dragon standards. Its capture would've been a real coup and a big payload for you."

"That's the same dragon who's been all over the newspapers this past week." Dr. Kenneth Westmore, a "Harvard man" he'd told Rudolph the first time they'd met, shifted his cagey green eyes away from the screen and to the men around the table. "Until this week, we could only speculate as to whether there existed a logical reason to the dragon's healing. We could never discern a pattern. They heal every race and nationality, both genders, all ages, and religions. They heal everything from dementia to kidney disease. No rhyme or reason."

As much as the Circle of Drayke studied dragon behavior, their haughtiness had prevented them from drawing the most obvious conclusion. Dragons hadn't survived for thousands of years because they were lucky. They'd survived because they were more intelligent and cautious than humans.

From the eyes of a trained soldier, the battle with the dragons proved illuminating. Once Rudolph stopped thinking of dragons as big flying snakes and more like thinking and feeling human beings with family and friends, his strategy became clear.

For the first time, the smallest of the dragons was on its own. That rarely happened, which, if the dragon was equivalent to a teenager in dragon society, meant two things. One, the older dragons were giving it a taste of independence. Two, with independence came limitations and oversight. That oversight had come in the form of an older and bigger dragon.

The big green dragon had responded to the helicopters the way a caring relative or friend would, it sought to protect. At first, by drawing one helicopter away. Lucky for Rudolph, he had another 'copter waiting for his directive. Once the pilot chasing the green dragon had radioed in, letting him know the gold dragon was alone, Rudolph had sent the second 'copter in.

Only three of his soldiers survived the crash into the ocean and the dragon's attack. Grainy as it may be, the video footage was salvageable, which was all the Circle of Drayke cared about. Rudolph still had calls of condolence to make.

Dr. Westmore, lean and fit and a man Rudolph wouldn't trust to write him a prescription no less operate on him, damn near salivated as he shared his thoughts.

"The gold dragon healed children dying from cancer. It didn't fly to any hospital to do it either. It went to hospitals with cancer centers. That shows thought, deliberateness, and purpose. Not random acts of healing, gentlemen. These monsters know precisely what they're doing." He slapped his palms on the table. "That's why we're here."

The men at the table nodded. Greed bloomed in their eyes.

"We'll have our dragon," Cafferty assured the group. "Once we do, we'll learn their secrets and steal their power. It's only a matter of time."

———※———

"No."

"Please, Father, it's been two months."

Kya walked beside her father through the Eshe Forest. With their golden scales, the dragons contrasted with the browns and greens of the forest. Gasira and Ledisi, however, who trailed behind them, blended almost to the point of camouflage.

"They tried to capture you."

"Yes, I know."

"If your sister hadn't destroyed the helicopters, they would've succeeded."

"I know."

"You almost drowned."

The giant golden dragon that was the Aragonite Star Dragon second and Kya's father first, stopped. At half her father's height and less than that his weight, she had to stare up to meet his eyes, a swirl of brown and red.

Her siblings halted as well, serving in the role of silent bodyguard, although nothing more dangerous than them called Buto home. Three-fourths the size of the United States, countless species of birds and insects lived on Buto along with a large population of deer, hippopotamus, wildebeest and elephants, which the dragons bred for food.

After the attack on Kya, her father had summoned every dragon home. For a month afterward, her siblings had searched for the origin of the helicopters. They'd had little evidence to guide their investigation. By the time they'd returned to the location in the Pacific Ocean where the helicopters had crashed, the men and the wreckage were gone.

Ever since, Kya has been banned from leaving the island.

A long neck caressed hers, a soothing back and forth that had Kya shifting toward the protective girth of her father.

"I won't allow the humans to have you. You're small, my Kya, even for a dragon of your age. Some humans, like the ones who attacked you and your sister, will think their technology superior and a small dragon easy prey."

Whiskers from a mouth pressed to her flank tickled. Her father used his forked tongue to determine the strength of her scales. His long, wide tongue ran from head to tail to legs before he repeated the movement on her other side.

"You're the Bloodstone Dragon. You're the prey of no human. With each passing century, humans develop more and greater weapons of war. As such, we must adapt. If your scales were less durable, their bullets would've done considerable damage."

They'd done damage enough. A furious and worried Ledisi had pulled Kya from the water and carried her home. Their mother, the Bluestone Dragon, had used the magic of her Lapis Lazuli stone to revive and heal Kya. When she slept, Kya dreamed of helicopters, nets, and scale-piercing bullets.

"You will train more, my Bloodstone Dragon. Make your scales impenetrable and your fire magic unstoppable. We may not prey on humans, and I may believe in healing the worthy among them, but that does not mean I will permit them to threaten my family."

The Aragonite Star Dragon stood to his full height of thirty feet, his length double that size, and looked over Kya's head and toward her oldest siblings.

Gasira and Ledisi snapped to attention without their father having to say a word.

"Small does not mean weak. I never want the Bloodstone Dragon to fear for her life because her elders have failed to prepare her for the world of humans. Train her better." His eyes, once more, fell to her. *"When you're ready, I'll permit you to return to the land of humans and your diata. Until then, listen to Ledisi and Gasira."*

Upon waking, Kya had confessed all. She hadn't liked lying to her parents any more than Ledisi had. There was no shame in befriending a human, although her father did not approve of her doing so while in dragon form. She'd assured them Armstrong Knight was an honorable man who would keep her secret.

Unless her father wanted to kill Armstrong to guarantee his silence, he had little choice but to accept Kya's judgment of the human.

Once she began her training and made noticeable progress, her father granted Kya a boon.

Flying high above Buto and beyond the protective mists of magic, Kya reached for and found Armstrong's mind.

I hope while I've been away that you haven't shocked any other female with your naked form.

Tension flooded her at the thought that her sudden reintroduction into his life, after months, would be unwelcomed.

If you're willing, diata, I can teach you how to speak to me telepathically. The magic involved requires absolute trust from the both of us.

A month. That's how long it took Armstrong Knight to master their dragon-human telepathic link.

It took Kya, however, much longer to make her "scales impenetrable" and her "fire magic unstoppable."

CHAPTER FOUR

ALL HE WANTED to do was make a quick deposit, scarf down a lunch of burger and fries, and then go home and get ready for work. Was that too much for a man to expect the day before Thanksgiving? A quiet, normal Wednesday? Armstrong guessed it was because three idiots who must've wanted to spend the next ten years in a federal pen pulled pump-action shotguns from their long leather coats.

Man, could these losers get any more cliché? He guessed they could because the men wore honest-to-goodness stockings over their faces. Squinted eyes, squished noses and mouths, if the men weren't cursing and waving their guns around and scaring the shit out of the tellers and customers, Armstrong would've laughed out loud. They looked that ridiculous.

But the situation and the danger everyone was in, including himself, was no laughing matter. The assholes may have been stupid because really, who in the hell robbed a bank nowadays, but they were about the greedy and deadly business of getting what they wanted.

Money.

Armstrong hoped the bank police officer, red-faced from anger and a bleeding nose he'd received when the tallest of the bank robbers sucker punched and disarmed him with embarrassing ease, wouldn't do something stupid and get himself shot. The man, who looked to be retirement age, probably thought a security detail at a bank an easy money gig. He didn't doubt it had been until the three clichés strolled in, shotguns out and demanding money.

"Get the hell on the floor."

Armstrong, who was second in line, followed the six other customers to the floor. Off-duty, he wasn't armed. Good thing he wasn't. If he were, he'd have an even larger dilemma. As it was, the reckless side of him wanted to take the men on. Fortunately, the trained Secret Service agent was in control, which had him planting his face to the floor and doing nothing.

"Put it all in the bag. Come on, we don't have all day. Hurry the hell up."

Only one of the men spoke, barking orders at the tellers while one served as lookout and the other was in the back with the bank manager.

"I said hurry up."

Armstrong chanced a glance upward. Twisting his head to the side, he could see the tall man, dressed in all black and leather coat like his partners, pace from one teller to the next. Two women and one man, Armstrong recalled when he waited in line. He held his gun at his side, the barrel pointing upward. It wouldn't take but a second for the bank robber, in a fit of anger or fright, to lower the weapon and shoot one of the tellers.

Turning his head a little more, Armstrong saw the black booted feet of the second man. He stood near the glass doors to the bank. Broad daylight. This brain trust had thought it a good idea to rob a bank in the middle of the day.

"Come on," the guy by the door yelled. "We can't be in here all goddamn day. Sooner or later someone else is going to want to come in. What am I going to do then?"

"All right, man. Damn. You heard him, hurry your asses up."

"Here. This is everything from the drawers."

He recognized the voice of the male teller. Armstrong hadn't liked the way the man had watched him when he'd entered the small neighborhood bank, as if he would, well, stick up the joint. He'd hoped, when it was his turn in line, the guy would have to wait on him. His money was as green as everyone else's and the color of a person's skin didn't determine their morality.

The teller's voice had trembled, but he'd spoken loud and clear. The unspoken message in his voice was just as clear: you got what you wanted, now get the hell out of my bank. He hoped the tall robber hadn't detected the same.

"Gotta little attitude, do you? Think you better than me?"

"Ah, no. But you got what you came for."

"So we can leave, huh? Is that what you trying to say?"

"You got the money. That's it. That's all I'm saying."

"Leave it. We don't have time for him. He's right, we got the money. Let's go."

Armstrong wished the tall man would take the lookout's advice.

Pop.

Shit. What the hell?

A child about five, who'd been quiet as his mother held him close, screamed and began to cry.

At the sound of gunfire, the security guard jumped to his feet.

No.

Pop. Thud.

Dammit.

More screaming, the tellers and customers.

The third man came running from the back, winded and talking fast.

"The fucker tripped the silent alarm. We gotta go. Now!"

"What about the safe deposit boxes?"

"In here." He jiggled a black bookbag at the tall robber, who hadn't moved from his spot in front of the tellers. "Let's go before the cops arrive."

"Gotta finish this."

Armstrong didn't like the sound of that. The male teller had been right. Why couldn't these assholes just take the money and leave?

He couldn't tell where the guard had been shot and he heard nothing from the vic in the back. If he had to guess, the bank manager was dead.

"There are too many witnesses. We can take care of them before the cops get here. No witnesses mean no one left alive to talk."

Even if he had his weapon, no way would Armstrong be able to take down three armed men before he got himself shot and killed.

"No, please," the mother behind him pleaded. "We don't know anything. We didn't see your faces. Please. Please."

All around him strangers cried and begged for their lives.

A third pop rang out, and Armstrong closed his eyes and gritted his teeth. He knew who'd been shot and by whom. He may not have liked the condescending teller, but the man didn't deserve to die.

"We're even. One apiece. Now let's deal with the rest of them."

The sound of guns being reloaded competed against the wild pounding of his heart and the rush of adrenalin.

Fight or flight.

Armstrong would fight.

He stood, and the three men turned to face him. Backs to the glass doors, the murdering bastards laughed when they saw him.

Armstrong planted his six-one, two-hundred-pound body of muscle between the mother and her child. None of them would survive this. But he wouldn't die on his stomach like a coward. His father had fought when his cancer had come out of remission. He hadn't gone down quietly and neither would Armstrong.

"Women and a child. It's just us men and these women and a scared kid." He raised his hands, letting them see he held no weapon. "Come on. No one else has to die today. You hold all the cards here. Got all the power." He spoke to the tall man, who still looked ridiculous in his stocking. If any of the three were in charge, it was him.

"Playing hero?"

He chuckled. "I'm no hero. I'm just a guy who wanted a burger and fries and didn't have a dollar to his name, so I stopped in here to cash my check." Armstrong pointed over his shoulder to the whimpering mother and son. "He's just a boy. If nothing else, let the kid go."

The lookout, a stout guy with dark-brown hair and a mangy beard, tugged on the tall man's sleeve. "Cops are coming. Leave it. We need to go."

The tall man couldn't leave it. He'd had plenty of opportunities to take the loot and flee the crime scene. His problem, which was also Armstrong's problem, was the man was more killer than bank robber.

He saw it now. Nothing he could say would talk the man down. His bluish-green eyes sparked with murderous intent.

The man raised his shotgun. Pointed it at Armstrong.

"This is what happens when you try to play hero."

For the rest of his days, Armstrong would remember what happened next because it shocked the hell out of him one minute and had him falling in love the next.

Get down, diata.

He ducked.

A metallic gold dragon's tail crashed through the glass doors, swiped in a short arc and lopped off three heads in a grisly smooth motion. Blood sprayed, heads flew, and bodies thumped to the floor.

"How is it you manage to find trouble wherever you go? Six months and I find you in yet another fight."

"In fairness, my actions both times were in defense of someone else."

Armstrong pushed to his feet and helped up the woman and her little boy.

"Are the police out there with you?"

He could hear sirens.

"They will be soon. I will take my leave."

Armstrong led the woman around the dead men and blood. She held her son in her arms, his legs wrapped around her waist and her hand pressing his head to her shoulder, whispering for him to keep his eyes closed.

The child didn't need to see the gruesome sight of three decapitated bodies. It was bad enough he'd have this awful memory that would likely replay in his nightmares.

It could've been worse, for them all. Armstrong was thankful Kya had the worst and best sense of timing. The dragon was a full day early for their date, but she was right on time to save his life and the life of everyone else in the bank.

My hero. I think I'm in love.

For six months, they'd done nothing but talk and get to know each other through their telepathic link. Most days he'd forget it was a dragon on the other end of the conversation. Armstrong had even created a human image of Kya in his mind, which made him feel less creepy for the feelings he was developing. But the fake human Kya in his mind didn't change the reality of their unorthodox relationship.

Exiting the building, the street flooding with DCPD, Armstrong could just make out Kya's gold dragon form in the chilly November sky. A dragon. He'd needed to see her to remind himself of what she truly was. If he ever forgot again, he had to only remember her reptilian tail severing the heads of the bank robbers. One clean slice. That was all it had taken.

She'd told him about the strength of her scales. When he'd felt how soft they were, Armstrong thought the dragon had exaggerated. He now knew differently.

"Tomorrow at midnight, Kya. Be on time."

"I'm the Bloodstone Dragon. I go where I please when I please."

Armstrong handed over the mother and child to one of the officers before digging in his coat pocket and pulling out his wallet and Secret Service special agent badge.

"Correct me if I'm wrong, but your father grounded you for more than six months. Literally."

"Admit you missed me, and I may forget the insult to my Dracontias pride."

He had missed her, which said a lot about his lack of a social life.

"Special Agent Knight," one of the officers said, "I need to take your statement."

Armstrong's eyes were still on the sky, although he could no longer see Kya.

"Of course. I'm coming."

The woman nodded and walked a few feet away and to another officer. Red-and-blue lights added light to the overcast day, but nothing could brighten the ugliness of the last half hour. The ordeal showed on the dazed face of each customer and employee who emerged from the bank.

"I'm glad you're back. And you know I missed you. Did you miss me?"

By the time Kya answered him, Armstrong had given his statement, checked on the mother and her son, and then gone home. He'd missed lunch and was late for work. He had a good excuse and one hell of a story to tell.

"What was there to miss, diata? Your blinding flashlight? Your purple drink? Your mockery and tiny inquisitive fingers?"

He laughed, and two agents, stationed at the White House gate with him, stared at Armstrong as if he were drunk.

"I'll take that to mean you missed me."

"I didn't miss you, Armstrong Knight."

"Yes, you did."

"No, I did not."

He waited. Twenty minutes later, his patience paid off.

"Fine. I missed you."

Armstrong grinned like a fool in love and couldn't care less about the looks the other agents shot him. Or the utter absurdity of nursing tender feelings for a dragon incapable of meeting his human needs.

Friendship was all that could ever exist between Armstrong and Kya. His mind understood. But he was having a hard time convincing his heart.

CHAPTER FIVE

SHE SHOULD FLY home. The past two years, Kya had spent much time in the land of humans. Specifically, she'd spent too much time in Washington, DC and with Armstrong Knight. So much time, in fact, her father had assigned her the North American region. Ledisi no longer flew with her to the United States, although they often met on the return flight home. Her sister, now that Kya had taken over the responsibility of North America, could resume her duties in South America.

Whether humans knew it or not, the Dracontias had divided up their lands into regions. The Aragonite Star Dragon assigned one or two dragons to each area. They cared for the humans with their healing magic when they could. They were neither beholden to the humans nor viewed their acts of kindness as a responsibility that dictated their lives.

Kya's second oldest sister, Jahzara, and her mate were the dragons assigned to North America. The large landmass had been their domain for over two centuries. With Jahzara's first hatchling on the way and a thirteen-month gestation period, the mated pair chose to relinquish the territory.

Now North America belonged to the Bloodstone Dragon. One dragon instead of two. Her father's faith in her humbled as much as it overwhelmed. What if she failed? What if she, the smallest and youngest of the Dracontias, couldn't live up to everyone's expectations?

The depressing thought had Kya changing direction and flying a path she knew all too well. Within minutes, the dragon hovered outside Armstrong's bedroom window. She knew his daily routine as well as she did the scent of the human and his various emotions. That's how, over a year ago, she'd managed to track him once entering the continental United States. His normal spice scent was mixed with fear and anger.

The foul combination had the Bloodstone Dragon speeding through the sky. While much may have angered Armstrong, particularly injustice, little frightened the male. When she'd landed in front of the building where his scent was the strongest, she'd heard and saw enough to know the dangerous humans from the innocent ones.

In hindsight, killing the three men may not have been strictly necessary. There were other options at her disposal. She hadn't liked the callous way they'd threatened Armstrong's life, even as he pleaded for the freedom of a child. Kya had never taken a life beyond that of sustenance. But this, the killing of humans, had nothing to do with sustenance or survival. As she watched Armstrong sleep, she understood it had been her own fear and anger that had prompted her to take the men's lives. A human shouldn't have such an effect on a Dracontias. Yet...

"How long do you plan on watching me sleep?"

"I did not wish to disturb your rest. I'm on my way home."

"Yet you're outside my window." Dark-brown eyes opened, and they stared through the open blinds and straight at Kya. *"I felt you when you arrived. What's the matter?"*

"I'm fine. I shouldn't have come."

Despite her words and common sense, she didn't fly away as she ought. Instead, she flew closer when Armstrong threw off his covers, got out of bed, and opened the window.

"There's my favorite dragon."

I'm the only dragon you know.

"You're still my favorite. Are you safe to touch?"

I am.

Kya stretched forward so he wouldn't have to lean too far out the window. Her head was too big to fit through the opening and Armstrong's arm too short to reach far. But they managed.

She said nothing as he stroked her face and neither did Armstrong. Kya relished the feel of his hand too much to ruin the moment with words better left unsaid. One of these days they would have to take partners, he a human wife and Kya a dragon mate.

Refusing to think of the future, Kya shifted as near to Armstrong as she could.

"How long will you be in Buto?"

I don't know. Jahzara's baby dragon has hatched.

"You're no longer the youngest dragon. Does that make you feel all grown up now, Auntie Kya?"

At three in the morning, you're not at all humorous.

"Guarding the president and the White House is serious enough. When I'm with you, I can relax and be myself. You don't care about trivialities, and you speak your mind, which is refreshing." The hand on her nose moved to her sharp fangs. "We're a strange pair."

We are indeed. Careful, diata, you don't want to lose a finger. Those aren't toys, and I cannot alter them the way I can my scales.

"Will you let me fly with you tonight? Tomorrow's my day off so I can stay up all night and be with you."

He'd asked her about flying together twice before. She'd scoffed at the suggestion the first time, thinking the request one of Armstrong's many jokes. The second time he'd asked, he'd done so with such sincerity he'd left Kya speechless.

Now, as his finger slid dangerously close to the tip of a fang, Kya questioned, once again, the power she allowed this human to have over her. His question, impolite and presumptuous, should've irritated her. No one rode atop a Dracontias, except a hatchling as young as Jahzara's little one. Dragons did not have riders. They weren't horses or camels. Her kind didn't ferry humans about, a tether around their necks for the dragon rider to control their tamed beast.

Armstrong's question was an insult to the Bloodstone Dragon. Yet to Kya, the human's friend, she saw the request for what it was, another way for them to connect and breakdown the barriers that separated the human Armstrong from the dragon Kya.

You don't know what you ask of me. Riding a dragon is simply not done.

"I know." Armstrong smartly removed his hand from her fang. "I just hoped that would be something we could share." His shrug didn't convince Kya of his nonchalance. "I trust you won't let me fall."

I very well may permit you to fall to your death.

"Is that a yes?"

It's a warning. You cannot live your life in both worlds. And neither can I.

"What does that mean?"

It means we have a friendship that shouldn't exist between our species. It means our desires are unnatural. It also means when our friendship draws to its inevitable end, the pain and loss will be greater than either of us can now anticipate.

"Well, aren't you a ray of dragon sunshine. Based on that doom and gloom future, we should end things right now. Is that what you want? For us to no longer be friends?"

You're frustratingly dramatic, Armstrong. I'm here because that's my choice.

"And I want you here, which is my choice. One day at a time. Don't ruin what we have today with negative possibilities of tomorrow."

Armstrong thought her young and naïve. Did he not see the same in himself?

Dress warmly, diata, and meet me on the rooftop.

Kya waited for Armstrong to close his window before she flew toward the building's roof. Ten minutes later, the door to the roof banged open. On the other side was a grinning Armstrong dressed in boots, pants, coat, gloves, and hat.

Winter was slowly giving way to spring. While DC nights were no longer frigid, the altitude Kya intended to fly was high enough to create a chill in a human.

"Now what?" Armstrong jogged toward her. "How do we do this?"

She crouched as low as possible. *Begin at my tail. It's the lowest point. Once on, climb until your chin is near the back of my head. Your arms are too short to wrap around my neck, and I refuse to use any sort of harness or tether.*

"I value my life too much to throw a rope around your neck. May I get on now?"

You may. And do be careful where you place your feet, knees, and elbows.

"Got you."

The man must've climbed trees as a child because the skill and speed at which he ascended her body was impressive.

"I knew you'd grown since the first time we talked on this roof, but I didn't realize how much."

I still have years before I'm at full physical maturity. I did have what you humans call a growth spurt. Are you comfortable back there?

"I don't know where to put my hands."

He squirmed. The weight of his body was negligible.

Having second thoughts?

"No. But I will admit the idea of riding you was less frightening in my head. Now that I'm up here, so high above everything, it's thrilling and scary."

If you're able to sit upright, I'll use my magic to secure your legs and hands. As long as you're in contact with my scales and magic, you will maintain your seat.

With a little more effort than had taken him to climb her, Armstrong was soon upright, his bottom on her neck and his palms on the top of her head.

Kya pushed Bloodstone magic through her scales. It rose, slithering bands of red magic that coiled around wrists, hips, and thighs. The bands of magic, to Armstrong, would look like crimson vines growing from her body.

This was as close as a human could get to a dragon and still live. He was, quite literally, bound to Kya. She felt that truth on a level deeper than the physical.

Too tight?

"No. I feel secure, but I can also move a bit."

Satisfied Armstrong was as safe as she could make him atop her, Kya took to the air. She heard his sharp intake of breath and then a ragged release.

"This is the most exhilarating and idiotic thing I've ever done. And I love it. This is amazing."

Kya kept her pace leisurely and her height relatively low. Flying too high or fast could kill Armstrong.

They flew over the Potomac River, Washington Channel, and the Tidal Basin. Kya flew as low as she dared, wanting Armstrong to experience the home of his birth from a different vantage point. Kya didn't know the names of all the buildings, but she'd spent enough time flying over the city to know where large numbers of visitors congregated.

The Lincoln Memorial. The National Mall. The Washington Monument.

"DC is beautiful at night and up here."

Capitol Riverfront. Georgetown. Adams Morgan. Chinatown.

Armstrong listed off the places he wanted to see from the sky. For hours, they flew, connected even when neither spoke.

Shaw. Anacostia.

By the time Kya returned to Armstrong's rooftop, the human was asleep. She uncoiled her magic and he didn't stir, not even when she called his name.

Kya summoned her magic, a fog of Bloodstone power. In the center of the dense fog, Kya shifted into her human form. She held an exhausted Armstrong in her arms. Floating over the roof and down to Armstrong's apartment window, Kya whispered a command and his window opened.

With precision, she managed to get them both inside his bedroom. Dispersing her magic fog, Kya placed Armstrong on his bed and went about removing his outer garments.

His sleeping face was peaceful and innocent. Sitting on the bed beside him, she gazed at him through the eyes of a human but with the heart and soul of a dragon. Kya yearned to touch Armstrong the way he touched her. The desire to do so was so strong Kya's hand raised to his face.

She stilled. What if he awoke? How would she explain? Worse, did she want Armstrong to awaken and see her in this human form? Naked and curious about his body and hers.

Kya's hand dropped to her lap. Coward. Her eyes fell closed, and she breathed him in, his natural spice scent and sweat from a long night of sightseeing.

The bed shifted, and Kya's eyes flew open. Armstrong Knight stared up at her, his eyes glassy from sleep.

"Beautiful," he whispered as if speaking to himself instead of Kya.

She wondered whether he was awake but was too afraid to find out. Kya didn't move.

"So damn beautiful. I wish you were real. I wish you could be like this all the time. A human. Or me like you. A dragon."

Without thinking, Kya pressed the palm of her hand to the side of Armstrong's cheek. Soft yet hard with a thin layer of whiskers.

He turned toward her palm and kissed it.

Kya had no words for how her body responded to that single action. The way her stomach clenched and heart raced. The way her body heated and ached.

He kissed her palm again, giving it a soft bite before withdrawing and closing his eyes again, a smile on his contented face.

Asleep.

Kya rose, surprised her unsteady legs held her. This could not happen again. Armstrong could never know her secret. If he did, he would ask, in that deceptively benign way of his, for Kya to be the human female of his dreams. Dragons could turn into a human, which didn't make them human. Magic, that's all it was. But Armstrong wouldn't understand. He'd view it as a rejection instead of the sacrifice it would be for Kya to make such a life-changing decision.

She wouldn't do it. Ever. Not even for the human she loved but shouldn't.

Calling her magic to her again, Kya refused to take a final look at Armstrong before she escaped through his window.

CHAPTER SIX

CAPTAIN RUDOLPH JUST had his ass handed to him by the Circle of Drayke. Did they think it was easy tracking a damn dragon? Did those pompous assholes think they could do a better job than Rudolph and his men? They could try to find another group of mercenaries who were willing to go up against magical monsters. They wouldn't find any better, and they damn well knew it.

He slammed down the phone receiver he still held in his hand. He'd taken the call in his study, away from his wife. He paid the bills. His wife didn't need to know exactly how.

They'd had him on speakerphone, which he hated. Real men did their business up close and personal, not behind faceless technology. That's what separated men like Rudolph from men like the Circle of Drayke. Rudolph understood real power could never be stolen. It had to be earned through hard work, grit, and sacrifice.

The Circle of Drayke wanted everything easy and fast, with no more effort on their part than writing a big fat check. Well, the real world didn't work like that. Capturing a dragon wasn't a simple task. It was damn near impossible.

He sighed, leaned back in his desk chair, and lit a cigar. For the last four years, he and his men had chased their tails. The gold dragon hadn't been as easy prey as he'd originally thought. After his men had almost captured the dragon, it had vanished. There'd been no sightings of the smallest dragon for months. In the days and weeks after the attack on the gold and green dragons, skies around the world had gone quiet with the absence of all dragons.

For him, this confirmed what Rudolph had suspected about the beasts. The creatures were intelligent, strategic even. At the first sign of danger, they'd gone to ground. They may not have known who was after them and why, but the dragons had taken precautions. Slowly, they'd returned from their hiding hole and taken to the skies, once again healing and helping.

The gold dragon, however, had taken much longer to return. When it did, to Rudolph's surprise, the dragon, still small compared to the others, was solo. The Circle of Drayke thought it the perfect opportunity for a quick snatch and grab. He'd disagreed. They'd argued.

He was overruled, and his men headed out. Mistake.

Flicking ashes in the tray, Rudolph swallowed the anger the memory evoked.

"All right, Turner, tell me what you see."

"The gold dragon is flying toward DC, Captain Rudolph. What's your order?"

"Is it alone?"

"Yes, sir."

Rudolph didn't like this plan. It felt wrong. Even with the new and improved dragon net, this op had the hairs on his arms sticking up. What bothered him was the fact that no other dragon flew with it. The big green dragon had downed, with frightening ease, two armored helicopters when the smallest dragon was in danger. If nothing else, Rudolph would've thought that dragon would be glued to the smaller dragon's side. Instead, the gold dragon flew the skies alone.

He hadn't survived this long without a backup plan. He may not have been up there with his men, but Rudolph was with them in spirit. From his basement, he had all the equipment he needed, care of the Circle of Drayke, to run a high-level secret operation. The US government didn't officially support the op, but the Circle of Drayke lined the right pockets and filled the right political coffers. American military forces wouldn't intervene, no matter how many bleeding-heart politicians sided with the so-called civil rights of dragons.

They were monsters, for Christ's sake, not people. They didn't have any damn civil rights to protect.

"Okay, listen up. I want that dragon reeled in tonight. We've been paid a lot of money, so let's earn every penny of it. Turner, you still got eyes on goldie?"

"Affirmative."

Captain Rudolph trusted every man under his command. They were military grade tough. But they were also flesh and blood and men with wives and children to get home to. He wouldn't have another incident like he did a year ago, which was why he'd talked the big ten into hiring more mercs for this mission.

"Smyth, Wilson, Hein converge on Turner's location now. The Golden Fleece is ours boys. Bring it down."

Rudolph listened, safe in his basement bunker, as his men went on the offensive. He smiled. This time tomorrow, he'd be a rich man. Not as wealthy as the Circle of Drayke, but few men were.

Men yelled over the radio as they pursued their prey. From the sound of things, the Golden Fleece wouldn't be taken easily. Rudolph expected as much, which was why he'd called in reinforcements. The dragon wouldn't be able to outmaneuver four state-of-the-art 'copters.

"What did you say, Turner? You're breaking up." He sat up in his chair. Was that a roar he heard? *"Turner, come in. Do you hear me?"*

Static crackled over the line but no Davis Turner.

"Smyth, do you have eyes on Turner's 'copter?"

"Shit. Where in the hell did that big fucker come from?"

"Smyth, what's going on? Somebody answer me."

On his feet, hand clutched around the radio, Rudolph could only listen and wait.

"Not alone."

"Two of them."

"Oh, god. Where did the other three come from?"

"Shoot 'em. Keep shooting."

Screams. All Rudolph heard were screams and nonsensical rambling.

"Wilson, Hein, come in. Tell me what's going on. Turner. Smyth."

"Fire, fire."

"Bullets useless. Bouncin' off. Damn, it's coming right us. R-right at—"

He'd once heard someone say hearing was worse than seeing because the mind's ability to conjure images was worse than anything the eyes could ever see. As Rudolph stood in his basement, safe and miles away from the aerial battle, he had no problem believing hearing was far worse than seeing.

What he heard, on the other line of the radio, were his men being slaughtered. Not simply dying but crushed by superior numbers and overwhelming power. Rudolph had known the op was a mistake. He'd told the rich bastards that it stunk.

Dragons weren't stupid. He knew that. But he'd moved against his better judgment and twenty good soldiers had lost their lives. There would be no rescue. The sounds of burning, roaring, and hissing assured him of that sad fact.

Slumping to the floor, the captain still held onto the radio. He'd failed. Again.

The gold dragon hadn't been prey but bait. And he'd swallowed the worm and line whole. Damn him and damn the Circle of Drayke.

Three years later, Rudolph hadn't gotten over the loss of so many men. More, the Circle of Drayke hadn't let him forget how much he owed them. They'd hired other men, more expensive than Captain Rudolph. But their track records were no better.

Sitting in his study, he knew they'd taken the wrong tact from the beginning. Dragons wouldn't be outmuscled, at least not without more firepower than Rudolph had at his disposal. Which meant they had to defeat them with brains instead of brawn. Meet their calculating minds with shrewd machinations.

The Circle of Drayke still wanted the gold dragon. At this point, stubbornness and pride fueled their decisions. They didn't care the dragon had gotten stronger and larger since their first encounter three years ago. They also didn't care public opinion polls favored the dragon. The beast was on every damn American magazine cover because it, unlike other dragons, focused on healing children.

Cigar smoke filled the air, the scent comforting and familiar. Randolph knew he was missing something. If he could only figure it out, everything would change.

Propping his feet on his desk, Rudolph considered what he knew about the gold dragon. One, it traveled between the United States, Canada and Mexico. Two, it healed children, although not exclusively. Three, it had no discernible route or favorite locales.

Wait, that wasn't true. His feet thudded to the floor. There was a pattern with the gold dragon. The one place it was spotted the most was DC. He'd forgotten. When the dragon finally returned to wherever it went after escaping his men, and their nets, witnesses from a bank robbery had told police a gold dragon had killed the bank robbers.

By the time DCPD had arrived on the scene, there was no dragon. But witnesses swore one had been there and helped them. For a while, Rudolph had investigated the event, hoping to find anything that would help him catch the elusive dragon. He'd hit a dead end. He couldn't figure out why a healing dragon would suddenly play a superhero. That wasn't their MO, so he'd let it drop.

Now, he wondered if he'd given up too soon. Maybe there was something there he'd missed. Getting to his feet, Rudolph moved to his file cabinet in the corner of the room. His wife complained he was a pack rat. He supposed she was right, his study and basement were overflowing with boxes and file cabinets.

He found the folder and notes on the bank robbery, employees, including the murdered ones, and the bank customers all of whom survived thanks to the gold dragon. Why would a dragon care about foiling a robbery? That's what he'd never understood about the case.

They healed. That was it. Except, for the gold dragon, that wasn't it. There was more, and Rudolph was going to find out what.

"Calling it a night?"

Armstrong returned his six-month-old niece to her proud father. Isaiah, hands big yet gentle, cradled Isabelle to his chest, her head on his shoulder and she fast asleep.

They sat in Isaiah and Nicole's living room on a Monday night, watching football and drinking beer. Well, Armstrong had a beer while his brother quenched his thirst on nothing stronger than iced tea. Since he'd become a father, Isabelle, the youngest of three girls, the bar owner had given up a lot of "vices," alcohol among them.

Armstrong didn't get it. It wasn't like Isaiah was a drunk. He rarely drank in excess or acted out the few times he did get drunk. But Isaiah, the oldest of the Knight children, had always taken his responsibilities seriously. Fatherhood was no different.

"You're a good dad."

"Where did that come from?"

"Just saying. You and Nicole are lucky. You got a good life and family. I'm happy for you."

With care to not wake the baby, Isaiah pushed off the couch and whispered, "Give me a sec. I'll be right back. Don't go anywhere."

Armstrong followed his brother to the steps that led to the upstairs. It was near the front door, the coat closet, and freedom. He loved his siblings and tried to visit them as often as he could. They were all married, even his youngest sister, who was as big as a house and expecting her second child. He, on the other hand, was still depressingly single.

He grabbed his coat from the closet and yanked it on.

"Don't you dare sneak out."

Armstrong's hand fell away from the doorknob. He thought he could slip out while his brother put the baby down to bed. Apparently not.

"You're fast for an old man."

"Old, huh? Just for that, I'm not going to step in the next time Nicole tries to set you up with one of her girlfriends."

Isaiah, three inches taller than Armstrong but not as muscular, was thirty-nine to his thirty-two. Glasses and a goatee had the man resembling their father. Isaiah had always looked more like their dad than any of the Knight kids. Except for his dark complexion, Armstrong favored his mother, who was two shades lighter than him and stunning at sixty-three. His father, like Isaiah, had chosen well.

Isaiah opened the front door, and they stepped outside. His brother left the door slightly ajar, adding illumination to a porch that already glowed from a security light.

"I guess you want to talk." It wasn't a question. Armstrong knew his brother.

"I'm worried about you."

"The job's fine. That thing with the terrorist the other day was—"

"You know that's not what I'm talking about. I'm used to your dangerous job. I want to know what's going on with you personally."

"You mean why haven't I settled down?"

Armstrong zipped up his heavy-duty coat. The only thing Isaiah had to keep him warm was his burgundy, gold, and white Washington Redskins sweatshirt.

"Yeah, that's what I mean. I know you want a family. I can see it every time you play with one of the kids. They all love Uncle Armstrong. You spoil them rotten."

"They're great kids."

He wanted a half dozen just like them.

"Tell me."

"I can't. Sorry."

"Can't or won't?"

"I'm a man of my word, Isaiah. I promised I'd keep her secret."

"The infamous and invisible Kya from a decade ago?"

More like seven years, but it felt much longer. He didn't answer his brother.

"Really? Come on, Armstrong. If she were the woman for you, you would've brought her around to meet all of us. You can't put your life on hold for a woman who doesn't make time for you and your family."

That wasn't true. Kya always made time for him. Isaiah was right, though. He had put his life on hold, which made no sense. He and Kya had no future. Armstrong knew that. He'd known from the start, and so had Kya. Yet they persisted in a friendship that was more intimate than any physical relationship he'd ever had with a human woman.

They told each other everything. He knew her and she knew him—his fears and insecurities as well as his mistakes and regrets.

His left hand in his pocket found his hat and Armstrong put it on. DC in December was damn cold.

"You must be freezing your balls off. Stop worrying about me and get inside."

"I'll stop worrying when you find a nice girl who'll take care of you."

"You sound like Mom."

Isaiah laughed. "Damn, I do, and I am freezing my balls off out here." Retreating to the threshold of his front door and the warmth of the house, Armstrong knew Isaiah watched him as he made his way off the porch and down the four steps to the walkway. "Do you love her?"

He answered without turning around. "I shouldn't, but I do."

"Does she love you?"

"She shouldn't, but I think she does."

He stopped and turned around, back to the street and front to his brother.

"If the two of you can't be together, which it seems you can't, for whatever reason, then you need to make a clean break. She moves on, and you move on. Drive safely, and I'll see you next Sunday at church."

Isaiah waved, then closed the door.

For several minutes, Armstrong remained on the sidewalk, staring at the white door and empty porch. Isaiah had gotten to the heart of the matter. It wasn't as if Armstrong hadn't known what needed doing. Hell, years ago Kya had made the same point as Isaiah. He'd been the one to ignore the obvious. If their friendship meant they'd never seek a suitable life partner, then maybe they needed to reevaluate their relationship.

He slid behind the wheel of his car, pulled into traffic, and began the short drive to Capitol Hill. He'd bought the house with hopes of having a wife and brood of children. Parking in front of it, Armstrong forced himself to admit he'd envisioned his dream Kya sharing the home with him.

Stupid. He'd wasted seven years on a fantasy.

"Kya, where are you?"

Getting out of the car, instinctively, Armstrong's eyes raised to the night sky. Quiet and still, he didn't see or sense the dragon.

"What's the matter, diata? You sound upset."

"We need to talk."

"Are we not speaking now?"

She hadn't told him where she was, which meant she was either on her way home or nearer than she wanted to admit.

The key in the lock had him opening the door and going inside. Whenever he went out and knew he wouldn't return until after dark,

Armstrong left a light on in the living room. It was a habit carried over from living with a mother and two sisters who worried.

The light in the living room was no longer on.

"I think someone's been in the house."

"Been or still in the house?"

He wasn't sure. But Armstrong wasn't about to stay there and find out. He backed up and heard the distinct sound of footsteps coming toward him.

"In the house. One. No, two."

"I'm on my way."

Unless Kya was right around the corner and intended to destroy his house to get to him, there was nothing she could do.

When the first punch came, it sent Armstrong on his ass. He couldn't see a damn thing, but he felt the kicks to his ribs and chest.

More than two men. They were strong and skilled.

He tried to get to his feet, but the men's fists and feet kept him down. They said nothing as they beat his ass.

He lunged at where he thought one of the assailants was, catching the man at his knees and bringing him down. He leveled three blind blows, grateful when his fists met face.

The satisfaction of getting some payback was short-lived. Two men grabbed him by his coat and pulled him off the other man. Rough hands dragged him toward his living room and tossed him onto his couch.

The light that should've already been on blinked to life.

Five men. Four big bruisers, one with a bloody nose, Armstrong noted with pleasure, glared down at him. It was the fifth man, however, who claimed most of Armstrong's attention.

Unlike the bruisers, he wore the smug smile of a man used to being in charge. Blond and dressed in a black trench coat, he sneered at Armstrong from a face that had known too many fist fights. Fifty-something and confident, he settled his forearms on his knees and pointed at Armstrong.

"It has to be you."

"What must be me, asshole?"

A punch to the side of his head had Armstrong gritting his teeth. During the fight in the foyer, his thick hat had come off, leaving him no protection against the strike. Payback was a bitch, and he would have his.

"You're the last one on the list. It didn't come when the others were in danger." The older man slid to the edge of the chair where he sat across from Armstrong. "For the longest time, I couldn't figure out why it had done it. Why it would even care. Then it came to me. It was protecting someone."

Armstrong had no idea what the man was talking about, although he feared it had something to do with the men in the helicopters who'd tried to kidnap Kya over the years.

He kept silent. Besides not wanting to get hit again, he wanted the man to keep talking. If this was about Kya, he needed to know.

"It makes sense. Dragons heal. Why wouldn't they also care to the point of protection?"

Damn, this was about Kya. These men couldn't have her. No way.

Stay away.

She didn't respond.

Do you hear me, Kya? I said stay away. False alarm. I'm fine. Go home. We'll talk tomorrow.

"We tracked them all down. We held them. Interrogated them. But no gold dragon. Either it no longer offers its protection or we had the wrong people. Which brings us to you, Special Agent Knight. You'll either prove my theory right or these last three years a waste of time and money."

The man, smaller than the others at five-ten, rose and went to the living room window. Pulling back the dark-green curtains, blue eyes looked out.

I'm fine, Kya. Just tired. Seeing things, you know. I'm going to bed now. Let's talk in the morning, and you can tell me what a fool I was tonight for making you worry for nothing. Go home.

"How do you do it?"

"Do what?"

"Bring it to you." Hands clasped behind his back, the man turned to Armstrong. "Tell me what I want to know, and we'll spare your life."

"I don't know what you're talking about."

"I think you do. You're not a very good liar. What will happen if we wait here? Will it come? Or maybe I need to have one of my men take a couple of fingers and toes. Would your screams of pain bring it to your side? Is that how it works? When you're in danger, the dragon comes?"

He didn't know what to say, so he went quiet again.

The man smiled, blue eyes twinkling when he nodded to the four men.

They jerked Armstrong from the couch, their fists connecting before he was fully upright. He fought back, striking any body part he could find. He'd neither hit so hard nor thrown so many punches. He also hadn't ever fought for his life the way he was now.

His coat was ripped from him as he struggled against the men.

By the time he collapsed to the floor, bloody and breathing hard, Armstrong could no longer raise his arms to protect or defend himself. They'd broken his nose and a couple of ribs, which explained the pain in his side and the labored breathing.

"Tell me what I want to know."

He wouldn't. These men would have to kill Armstrong before he betrayed his dragon.

"Go to hell." The blood in his mouth was spat on the shiny black boots that hovered near his head. "And get the fuck out of my home."

The older man laughed and raised his booted foot over Armstrong's bloody and swollen face. "If you're dead, will it come? I guess I'll find out."

A gust of wind swarmed into the room, toppling the men. The blond man tumbled backward, swatting at the red fog that accompanied the wind. The four bruisers were also caught up in the fog.

Armstrong couldn't see what had the men ensnared, but he knew it had to be Kya's magic. He'd never seen it like this before, but he felt her presence in the room.

The men screamed from inside the red fog. That was all Armstrong heard. The sound of five men captured, desperate, and in horrific pain.

Armstrong struggled to his feet. Limping, he made his way around the couch and away from the fog.

"Are you all right, Armstrong?"

"Kya? Is that you inside the fog?"

Although, he didn't see how it could be. But it was her voice who'd spoken, different yet similar to how she sounded in his head.

"Who else would it be?"

Yeah, that smart mouth was his dragon.

"How can you fit in that fog? And how come I can hear your voice outside of my head?"

"Do you wish me to kill them?"

"I thought you already had."

"Close, but they still breathe. I can change that if it's your wish. They deserve to die. I can smell your blood."

Kya was an all or nothing dragon. For her kind, gray didn't exist.

"Don't kill them. But don't heal them, either."

Whatever she'd done to the men, Armstrong figured they deserved at least that much.

"Kya, how are you in my home?"

"It doesn't matter. I'm here, and you're safe. I will take these humans far away from here."

The red fog shifted, and so did Armstrong.

"No, no. Don't you dare. Tell me. Show me what you're hiding."

"No."

"Dammit, Kya, show me."

Years ago, he'd had a dream about Kya. It was the night they'd first flown together. He'd fallen asleep on her back. When he'd awoken, he'd been in his bed. Armstrong could never reason how the twenty-five-foot dragon had gotten him into bed without destroying his home. No more than he'd ever been able to figure out how she managed to enter his apartment that first night.

The fog moved toward him. Men fell out and onto the floor. No cuts or bruises, only those he'd managed to get in when they'd fought. What had she done to them?

"This isn't done."

So she said every time they ripped away one more layer that separated dragons from humans. Armstrong thought they had no secrets between them. He'd been wrong.

The fog dispersed. In front of him stood his dream. Bronzed, beautiful, and naked. Dark spirals of hair cascaded over shoulders and to waist. Hips flared out and long legs went on forever. Breasts, full and large, were formed to succulent perfection. For all her outward beauty, the green jasper eyes had his heart clenching.

Armstrong reached for her. With only a second of hesitation, she came, drawing him to her on a sob.

Or maybe it was he who cried. With joy and renewed hope. Tonight, he'd been prepared to break his heart by giving her up. Now, with Kya's secret out in the open, he wouldn't have to.

"My gorgeous Bloodstone Dragon. You're human."

CHAPTER SEVEN

AS MUCH AS Kya despised the scent of Armstrong's blood, the feel of his arms around her had her stomach roiling for all she'd yearned for his touch and the years of self-denial. She despised that, too, her weakness and need for this human.

"I can't believe you're human." His arms tightened and, if possible, he held her even closer. "You shouldn't have come. I'm grateful you did, but you shouldn't have come."

"They would've killed you if I hadn't. Do you think yourself better suited to handle five men than a dragon?"

His laughter rippled through him and against her human chest.

"You're the same, no matter the form. Let me get a good look at you."

He released her and stepped back. She thought his eyes would fall to her nude form. Instead, his dark eyes never left hers.

"You're bleeding."

"You're beautiful."

She had no words. Dragons weren't beautiful. She'd seen herself in her human form many times, although she rarely made the shift. Kya had no concept of self-beauty. Yet, whenever she looked upon Armstrong, Kya thought him lovely. His beauty came from the soul and heart of the man she knew so well.

For Armstrong, apparently, her beauty came only in the form of a human female. Did that make him shallow, as she knew most humans to be? Or did it make him all-too-human, capable of appreciating what pleased his eyes as well as his mind?

Kya had no idea. Being in this body, with Armstrong's heart in his eyes, she could hardly breathe, no less think.

"Let me heal you, diata. Then I will take care of the humans."

Using the sleeve of his shirt, Armstrong wiped the blood from his mouth and nose with a pained slowness that had Kya shifting back to the unconscious men on the floor. She should kill them. Magic thrummed through her body, red-hot and lethal. Even in this form, it would take little effort to end the threat to Armstrong's life.

"Don't."

"Why not?"

"They aren't worth it."

She disagreed and took two steps toward the humans. A strong arm wrapped around her waist, Armstrong's body pressed close.

Too close.

"I can't explain five dead men in my living room to the police. Unless you're an expert at disposing of bodies, you shouldn't kill them."

"We eat our prey. Don't allow this form to cause you to forget what I truly am."

The palm of his hand flattened on her stomach. Caressed.

Kya wished he wouldn't do that, wished even more his touch didn't make her human body feel so good and needy.

"I could never forget the Bloodstone Dragon that is Kya. But you don't eat humans. And I don't want you making an exception for me."

The nose that rose to nuzzle her hair had Kya, quite disgracefully, leaning back into his warm embrace. "You should've told me. I understand why you didn't. But God, Kya, this is one hell of a secret you've been keeping."

"If Father knew I revealed myself, I would never be allowed to leave Buto. Worse, he would kill you." The thought had her pulling away from Armstrong. Conjuring clothes, which she should've done instead of permitting him to lay hands on her naked body, Kya turned around to face him. "Do be quiet so I can heal your injuries."

Thankfully, Armstrong obeyed. It was a brief respite. As soon as she dealt with the damage to his body and the men who harmed him, Armstrong Knight would push. It's what he did. She'd never liked that aspect of his personality because it brought out the worst in hers. She relented far too easily, a weakness unbefitting a Dracontias.

"Feel better?"

"Much. Thank you." He touched his nose, which had been broken in two places. "It's back to normal, and I can breathe just fine now. My ribs are good, too." He moved his arms and legs, testing his body, she supposed.

"You are as you should be. You'll find no lingering ailments. I take offense you think you would."

"You always take offense. Too much pride isn't good."

"I assume that assessment also applies to you."

"If it'll make you feel better, then yes." Bold, brown eyes traversed her sheathed form. "You look really good in jeans and that red silk shirt is sexy as hell. You make a man want to eat you up."

"You want to eat me?" She didn't understand. Armstrong wasn't a cannibal.

"You have no idea how much."

She stepped away from him.

"Wait." He laughed. "You misunderstand. I didn't mean it literally." A scratch to his head. "Well, I kinda did. But it's still different from what you're thinking."

"I think I've never understood you less. I didn't detect brain damage when I scanned you for injuries. So I assume you're brain is functioning properly and you're just exhibiting your normal strange behavior."

"There are so many things I want to say and ask you. But we need to take care of those men."

Kya had questions of her own, beginning with why the men were at Armstrong's home and why he lied about it being a false alarm. She hadn't believed him, of course. For some reason, he'd wanted Kya to stay away from his home and these men. Yes, she had many questions.

"We need to take them somewhere." Going from one man to the next, Armstrong searched them. "I need to know who they are. Their wallets will help with that." He scanned what he'd taken from the men. "Driver's licenses. Perfect." Returning the wallets to the men, Armstrong kept five plastic cards and secured them in a wooden desk in his living room. "Can you help me without turning back into a dragon?"

"I don't like the way you said that. As if my dragon form is less than my human one."

"That's not what I meant. I think you're trying to start an argument to give yourself an excuse to shift and fly away to Buto without us talking about the very big elephant in the room."

"There's no elephant in the room, big or otherwise."

"It's a metaphorical idiom, which you know. I also think you pretend to not understand me as a form of annoyance and avoidance. You're the smartest person I know."

"I'm not a person. I'm a dragon."

He threw up his hands. "See. That right there. That's what I'm talking about. Tell you what, I'm going to run upstairs and take a quick shower. You, Bloodstone Dragon, can take care of removing those assholes from my living room. And Kya, don't run away."

"You have no sway over any of my decisions, Armstrong Knight. As I once told you, I will go where I please, when I please, and in whichever form I please."

"You just added the bit about the form." An index finger tapped his temple. "I may not have your perfect memory, but I recall everything you've ever said to me. It was a request, not a command. We really need to talk, and I'd rather not do it in torn clothes and dried blood."

"And you'd rather have that conversation while I'm in this form?"

"I didn't say that."

He didn't have to.

"Go. Shower. I'll be here in your preferred form when you return."

Armstrong opened his mouth, shut it, and then marched out of the living room. Which left Kya alone with five humans and her thoughts.

------◦◦◦------

Armstrong stood at the top of the stairs. He had to play this right or Kya would fly out of his life and never return. The shower had done its job, giving him uninterrupted time to plan next steps. Maybe he should've let Kya kill those men. It would go a long way to solving his dilemma.

The fact that they hadn't taken precautions to conceal their identity said a lot to Armstrong. Not only had they revealed their faces, but the men also carried government-issued identification. Combined, those two facts could mean only one thing. The men had intended on killing him. The older man said Armstrong was the last person on his list from survivors of the bank robbery. Come tomorrow, he would begin his own investigation. He needed to know the extent of the threat to Kya.

Were the five men it, or were they the tip of a dangerous dragon hunters' iceberg?

Still, Armstrong wasn't a murderer, and he wouldn't turn Kya into one by using her natural protective dragon instincts to get what he wanted. What Armstrong wanted, for seven long years, was Kya. That dream was now within reach, and Armstrong was surprised how far he was willing to go to make it his new reality.

Armstrong had never lied to Kya. That wasn't the type of relationship they had. Now, as he strolled down the steps, sweatpants and a T-shirt on, Armstrong was prepared to fight for what he wanted.

"What did you do with them?" He honestly didn't care. What he did care about was that Kya was in his home, on his couch, and still in human form. "You don't look as if you're about to throw up, so I guess you didn't eat them."

She eyed him with an unreadable expression when he joined her on the sofa. In this form, Kya was no more forthcoming with her feelings, although he felt better able to read her emotions now that she had features he was used to deciphering. As a Secret Service agent, Armstrong had a lot of practice in interpreting verbal and non-verbal cues.

Right now, back to the cushions, arms crossed over her chest, green jasper eyes stoic, Kya was trying to close herself off. That wouldn't do.

He slid one cushion length closer. "Where are they?"

"Kerguelen Islands."

"Ker-what?"

"Southern Indian Ocean. Remote. The closest population area is over two-thousand miles away. There are no more than a hundred or so residents at a time, depending on the season."

"You left them on a deserted island?"

"The territory is known as Desolation Islands. That's not the same as deserted. For your peace of mind, I also healed them so they wouldn't die, although they still may if they don't make friends with the locals. Based on how they mistreated you, I doubt they know how to treat anyone, even if it means their survival."

Oh, but his dragon had a wicked streak.

"That's pretty ruthless of you."

"I'm a dragon. How many times must I remind you?"

"You're a kind and sensitive dragon, Kya. Stop pretending as if you enjoy when you act out in violence or vengeance. I know you don't, which was why I asked you to not kill them." He slid even closer, invading her personal space, which he knew she hated. "Are you mad at me?"

"Tell me why those men were in your home."

"Tell me how you look like the Kya of my dreams. I mean, you look exactly the way I envisioned you would if you were human. How is that possible?"

"It isn't, and you're far too close."

"Am I?" When Armstrong leaned in, his left arm pressed against her right and his lips were inches from her face. "You're the woman from my dreams. I had no idea you shifted into anything, no less a human. But I saw you, this human you, years ago. When I dreamed, you came to me, and I thought you were a figment of my imagination. But you weren't."

"Armstrong, I—"

He kissed her. Short and sweet and on shocked lips. It wasn't his best move, but he had to taste her. If he'd asked permission, she would've said no.

"You shouldn't have done that."

"I know."

He did it again. This time, he moved in slow, giving Kya time to push him away if she didn't want his kiss. Perhaps she was still in shock, but she didn't move, say no or shove against his chest. So he kissed her again. Nothing fancy. Just a press of lips to lips. She wasn't ready for more, wouldn't even know what more was because Armstrong had no doubt Kya had never allowed any human to touch her like this before.

The knowledge of her complete innocence and trust had him whispering his greatest secret.

"I love you, Bloodstone Dragon. Kya." He wanted to know if she loved him in return but stopped himself from asking. Armstrong didn't want to spook her more than he probably already had. "Stay with me tonight. I'm not asking you to commit to more than sleeping at my side.

Of letting me hold you while you sleep and being here when I wake up."

"This can never be. *We* can never be. Even if I let you hold and treat me like a human woman, I can never be her for you. Your love is wasted on a dragon's heart."

Armstrong kissed her again because she was right and painfully wrong. Cradling her face between his hands, he showed Kya, without words, how to kiss. Lips moved against hers, slow, soft and patient. To his delight, Kya was a fast learner. She responded with aching tenderness and desire.

God, he wanted to deepen the kiss, wanted to slake his pent-up urges and make Kya his in every way possible. He wouldn't, no matter the temptation. Not only was Kya a virgin, but she also wasn't ready for that level of physical intimacy. He didn't even think she understood her human body enough to know what she was feeling and why.

Lips slid to the long column of her neck. Mouth opened and tongue came out to explore. She gasped, and he did it again. A hand found nape, hair, and scalp. Another moan.

Damn, Kya was so responsive. And innocent.

Forcing his hands and lips to obey, Armstrong gave Kya one last peck on her lips and moved to the other side of the couch.

Dazed, she stared at him as if she didn't know what to say or do. They sat there while Kya made out whatever was on her mind. Armstrong, too afraid to tip the balance in the wrong direction, chose to keep his mouth shut.

"You're going to break my dragon's heart, Armstrong Knight."

"I promise, I won't."

"You will because I want what isn't mine to have. I cannot live the life of a human."

"I didn't ask you to."

"The question was in your gentle kisses, your reverent hands, and the eyes that gaze upon me with conflicted hope."

"One day at a time. Tonight, we share the same bed. Not as new lovers but as old friends."

"Tell me why those men were here."

He should've known his dragon would return to that topic.

"I think it had something to do with the terrorist threat against the president."

"Why did you ask me to stay away?"

"We aren't supposed to be connected, remember? I didn't want you swooping in here and lopping off heads."

Armstrong wondered if, since she wasn't in her dragon form, Kya could smell his lies. If she could, he would lose her for sure. When she nodded, he smiled at his success. Then frowned on the inside. He hated lying to her almost as much as he loathed the thought of losing her. What did it matter anyway? Those men, after getting a taste of Kya's magic, wouldn't come back for more. Only fools would challenge a dragon.

Or lie to one, he thought, guilt robbing him of the pleasure of potentially having Kya stay the night.

"What if they return?"

"They won't. I think it's safe to say you scared the crap out of them. They won't come back."

"Will you call to me if they do?"

"Yeah."

He wouldn't. Armstrong had a good idea why the men wanted his Kya. He'd be damned if he let anyone lock her in a cage, use her as a weapon of war, or experiment on her for their sadistic pleasure of taming a dragon.

The next time they came for Armstrong, thinking to use him to get to Kya, he'd be ready for them.

Taking Kya by the hand, Armstrong led her up the stairs and to his bedroom. She watched him as he undressed her to her underwear and said nothing when he removed her bra and replaced it with one of his T-shirts.

Gorgeous dragon eyes on him, Armstrong yanked off his T-shirt, socks, and pants. In his boxers, he climbed into bed and raised his hand to Kya.

She didn't move. "This is a mistake. I'm not a human."

"I fell in love with you as a dragon. This isn't about being human or dragon but our feelings for each other."

He lowered his hand and snuggled under the covers. Kya knew her mind. As she'd told him many times, she did as she wished.

"Do not think I don't know when I'm being emotionally manipulated."

"As I said, you're the smartest person I know, as well as the stubbornest. You make me work for every inch you give."

"That's because you want too much."

"I only want you."

"As I said, you want too much."

With a dip of the mattress, Kya joined him. A statue would've been softer for all that she didn't relax.

"Come here, my Bloodstone Dragon."

She didn't, so Armstrong moved to her. With a bit of effort, he managed to convince Kya to lay on her side. Spooning behind her, he held her the way he'd dreamed of for years. For once, they were the same size and Armstrong felt like her equal.

"I love you, Kya. I don't care if you're dragon or human. My feelings for you will never change."

"I won't say it back. I cannot."

"I know, sweetheart. I know."

She twisted in his arms until she faced him. Then kissed Armstrong, inexperienced and a little shy. Whatever the dragon felt for him, that went unvoiced, was expressed in her single kiss.

CHAPTER EIGHT

*"**IT WAS A** mistake."*

"Yes, so you've said."

Kya and her mother, the Bluestone Dragon, hovered far above their island home. Four different shades of green comprised her mother's scales, beginning with light-green at her tail and increasing in richness as the scales moved up her body and closer to her head and face. Her eyes, blue mottled with white, shone brightly with the color of her healing stone, Lapis Lazuli, as well as a mother's disappointment in her youngest offspring.

"You've revealed the second greatest secret of the Dracontias. The first being the magic stone in our skull. Does your human know that secret as well?"

"No. I would never."

"Until twenty minutes ago, I would've also thought you incapable of being so careless. Yet, you were. We watch and we learn, Kya. We

can also befriend if needed. There's no shame in finding and learning from a diata. Over the years, your father and I have found many a worthy human who've aided our knowledge of their modern world."

Her mother flew away from Buto and Kya followed. Though not as large as the forty-foot Bluestone Dragon, Kya could keep pace. Well, she could as long as her mother wasn't flying at her maximum speed, which she rarely had reason to do.

This flight, which humans would refer to as a stroll, had nothing to do with a dragon's aerial prowess but a daughter's confession and a mother's wisdom.

"A dragon's heart is pure. Our healing magic makes it impossible for us to act on anything but the most genuine of emotions. Your magic sought your human in his dreams. Showed him the human part of the dragon you keep hidden inside."

"I didn't intend for that to happen, Mother."

She'd revealed her second form to Armstrong through dragon dream magic. A mistake she hadn't realized she'd made until a month ago.

"Where the conscious mind refuses to act, our stone magic will bring forth our heart's desire when we slumber. When you slept, you dreamed of the human. When he slept, he dreamed of you. Your Bloodstone merged the two unconscious desires until they actualized on the physical plane and the conscious level. Not a mistake, daughter, dragon mate magic."

Dragon mate magic? Kya stopped. Her mother didn't. She circled Kya, gliding the light-green tip of her tail around Kya's head and neck.

Around and around she went, caressing Kya's scales and calming her runaway heart. A dragon hadn't bonded with a human in hundreds of years. All had left Buto, choosing to live in the land of the humans as a human. And all had returned with offspring from the union.

Kesins. Two-legged dragons with no Dracontias healing stone in their skull, no magical powers and no flight ability. These land dragons were half the size of Afiya, full-dragons, and didn't possess a gold to green color scale but a red to yellow range. While they could shift, they had far less control over their transformation than a full-bloodied dragon.

Kesins, regardless of whether the mother was human or a dragon in human form, was always born as a human. Within six months of a Kesins birth, however, they would shift for the first and final time. They had no magic to stay as a human and live among them. So the dragon parent would return, Kesin in tow, to Buto, leaving behind their human mate.

She'd never heard of a dragon-human mating that lasted beyond the birth of a Kesin. Dragons cherished their mates but loved their offspring more.

"Follow your heart, Kya. It has already chosen. You will not be fully happy on Buto if you fail to answer the question you cannot escape."

"What question is that?"

The Bluestone Dragon halted in front of Kya. Face slid beside hers and rubbed with a mother's affection.

"What if. Life, my daughter, is full of what ifs. The more of them we possess, the less happy we are with our choices. The larger and more significant the what if, the harder it is to look forward instead of backward. Seek the answer to your heart's desire."

"My heart is here."

Her mother resumed flying, and Kya followed. Not a staid pace this time. In an hour, they were over the Eastern Seaboard of the United States.

"Your heart is also here. Find the answers you seek. Home will always be there when you need it."

"What if I return home with a Kesin?"

"The Dracontias will love your Kesin as we love the others. Your father eschews dragon-human pairings because the sacrifice for the dragon is great. But your father has never known how it feels to have his heart pulled in two different directions, which makes him protective of the Dracontias to the point of narrow-mindedness."

"It won't last. Why should I try?"

"We live long lives, daughter. Too long to nurse what ifs and re-grets."

"And too long to nurse a broken heart."

"True. The decision is not an easy one. But it's yours to make, not mine or your father's."

Green scales rubbed gold before her mother flew away. The Blue-stone Dragon flew at a leisurely pace, glancing back once to see if Kya followed.

She should follow. Kya wanted to return home with her mother and to the easy life of a dragon unencumbered by unnatural desires and thoughts of a doomed mate bond.

She should follow, but she did not. Instead, she watched her mother fly farther away until she could no longer see the green scales of home and safety.

Reminding herself she was the Bloodstone Dragon, Kya shored up her nerves and went in search of her human.

Armstrong found himself tapping his foot every five seconds, run-ning fingers through his short hair every ten seconds, and glancing at the front door of the restaurant every twenty seconds. He was ridicu-lous. Yet there he sat, in the best steakhouse restaurant in DC waiting for his dragon-human date.

"Ah, look at him Isaiah, Armstrong's so cute when he's nervous." His sister-in-law laughed, a mocking sound that had him glaring at Ni-cole. "What? You're adorable. In all the years I've known you, I've never seen you nervous before. It's kind of sweet."

"It's not sweet." Isaiah, who sat beside his wife and across the table from Armstrong, shook his head. "It's pathetic. Look at you, you ha-ven't said more than ten words since we sat down and you keep staring at that damn door. You know, a watched pot never boils."

"That's a stupid saying." Needing something to do other than, yes, stare at every customer who came through the restaurant door, Armstrong downed his glass of water.

What made him the pathetic loser his brother accused him of being was that he was sweaty, anxious, and acting like a complete idiot and Kya wasn't even late. In fact, Armstrong, Isaiah, and Nicole were fifteen minutes early. Yet, Armstrong had a right to his anxiety. After the big reveal and the platonic night they'd shared in his bed, Kya had shifted back into her dragon form and flown away the next night.

She'd stayed away for a month. Not away from North America and the children she loved to heal and help but away from Armstrong. They'd connected telepathically, but the conversations were awkward when they'd never been before. Then, two weeks ago, she'd returned. For days afterward, he'd watched the sky for a big ass gold dragon in the form of Kya's father.

She'd laughed but didn't tell him he was being paranoid. Most nights they shared his bed and some mornings he awoke with Kya by his side. She didn't speak much, and he didn't push or complain. Kya, as she reminded him, was a dragon, which meant Armstrong could never have the kind of relationship with her that his brother had with Nicole.

That was okay. He'd take his dragon however he could have her. This double date was Kya's first real interaction with anyone in a social setting outside of Armstrong. She'd agreed to meet his family, though with a lot of reluctance on her part and pleading on his. That was two days ago, and he hadn't seen or heard from her since.

"Listen, Kya's shy and doesn't talk a lot so try not to overwhelm her."

Nicole, pretty in a navy-blue fitted dress, smiled at Armstrong. About a year ago, when she was pregnant with Isabelle, she cut her hair into a short, classy style. She now wore it in choppy layers that were combed and teased to the front and fell over her forehead in bangs.

"I guess opposites do attract. I can't believe you went out and found a quiet girlfriend."

Armstrong wouldn't dare define Kya as his girlfriend, but Nicole was right about opposites attracting. More than she would ever know.

"My point is that our family can be a bit much. She's more subdued than us."

"If she can deal with you, then she's not fragile. Relax," Isaiah said. "You're making way more out of this than is necessary. I already like the woman. If for no other reason than she got you on hooks and got Nicole and me out the house. Thank God for grandmothers who like to babysit. Do you hear me? Are you even listening?"

He wasn't because the woman of his dreams had just walked into the restaurant. Damn but she was gorgeous. Shiny, dark hair was piled atop her head in an elegant twist style. Tendrils flowed down the long column of her neck and onto well-defined shoulders. Spaghetti straps held the sexy form-fitting black dress in place. The mouth-watering garment fell to Kya's ankles and, God help him, it hugged every voluptuous dip and curve of her body. The dress tempted for all that it hid yet alluded to.

The next time Kya claimed she didn't know anything about being a human female, Armstrong was calling bullshit and shutting her down. Because, yes, his dragon knew how to make one hell of an entrance. Kya had style. He'd known that the first time she'd conjured clothing. But he had no idea how well she could put herself together when she set her mind to it. Maybe he wasn't the only one nervous and wanting to make a good first impression.

Instead of waving her over, Armstrong pushed from the table and hurried over to her. Not that she would notice or care, but he didn't like so many male's eyes were on her.

As he approached, Kya smiled and nodded, acknowledging him in that regal way of hers.

He didn't know how he should greet her. They'd never done this before, meeting in public and Kya as a human. They had no reference point, which brought back his butterflies.

"Do stop staring, Armstrong. I feel self-conscious enough without you gaping at me like a fish caught in a sailor's net."

Her dragon tongue. He loved it. Armstrong laughed and pulled Kya in for a quick hug and kiss on the cheek.

"You're a sight for sore eyes. I didn't know if you would show up." He released her then claimed her hand, lacing his fingers through hers and turning toward the table where he'd left Isaiah and Nicole.

"I assume you don't mean your eyes are literally sore."

"I don't, so no healing magic required."

By the time they maneuvered around tables, diners and waiters, Nicole and Isaiah were standing. Still a little nervous but feeling better with Kya by his side, Armstrong made introductions.

Kya, at six feet, towered over the five-five Nicole, who greeted the dragon with a warm hug and a, "It's nice to finally meet you."

"It's definitely nice to meet you, Kya." Isaiah shook her hand. "For a while, I thought you were a figment of my brother's imagination. But nope, you're as real as the rest of us."

Kya was real, just not a real human.

Armstrong held out Kya's chair, and she sat. He followed, unable to keep his eyes off her. His dragon was stunning in her human form, and he felt lucky and honored she'd chosen him.

When they picked up the menu to order, Armstrong realized he'd never seen Kya eat a single thing while in human form. He'd cooked them breakfast, and he'd eaten. In his happy state at having Kya in his home, Armstrong hadn't paid attention to her lack of appetite. He'd made reservations at the steakhouse because he knew Kya was a carnivore. But devouring a wildebeest as a twenty-five-foot dragon wasn't the same as eating a ribeye steak as a human. Did wildebeest even count as red meat?

Hell, why didn't any of this occur to him before now?

Kya ordered wood grilled kohlrabi steak, vegan paella, asparagus, and fennel-roasted onion.

"Where in the world did you find a vegetarian dish on a steakhouse menu?" Isaiah asked.

Armstrong tried not to gape. He was sure Kya would order the bloodiest steak allowable under the FDA.

"I only consume meat once a month. It's all my body requires. But Armstrong insists on filling my breakfast plate with bacon, sausage, and something called scrapple. I didn't want to know what animal scraps comprised the side dish, so I refused to ask."

"Wait, my brother cooks you breakfast?"

"If one considers what he does cooking, then yes. It's thoughtful but quite unnecessary."

Isaiah and Nicole looked at each other and then burst into laughter.

"You could've told me you didn't like my cooking."

"For me to dislike your cooking, I would've actually had to taste the food. Which I was disinclined to do."

His brother and sister-in-law continued to laugh, their eyes ping-ponging from Kya to Armstrong.

He should stop. This wasn't the time or place to get into an argument with his dragon.

"Do you have any idea how early I have to get up to cook for you, or how long it takes to get the scrapple just right so it's crisp but not overcooked?"

"Yes, from start to finish, forty-five minutes."

"That was a rhetorical question."

"Was it?"

She damn well knew it was.

"Oh, yeah," Isaiah began, "she's a real introvert. I've never seen anyone shier."

Under the table, Kya grabbed his hand and held it. It trembled, although none of the rest of her did. His heart constricted with love for his Bloodstone Dragon. Like he'd been earlier, Kya was nervous. Unlike Armstrong, she hid it behind a dragon's pride.

For him, she made an effort. She smiled and talked and answered questions with as much honesty as their situation allowed. She peppered lies with the truth, which had his heart constricting for another reason. To be together, they would always have to lie.

By the end of the evening, Armstrong could sense the strain of the night on Kya. When she chose to meet him at home instead of riding in his car, he knew she needed to cast off her human shell and take to the sky in her natural form.

He didn't take it personally when Kya slid into bed at dawn. Armstrong simply scooted to her and held his dragon close. There was still much to learn about Kya, the dragon and the human. One thing he knew about both was that Kya took comfort in physical contact.

Armstrong wondered if that was a Kya thing or a dragon thing. Something in the way she burrowed against him, her arms going around his back and caressing, even when she slept, made him think this was the way dragons showed their love and affection.

That dinner turned into a five-year unorthodox relationship. All the Knights loved Kya, especially the children. She doted on them in that quiet yet commanding way of hers. His mother loved her but didn't like the idea of them "shacking up without the sanctity of marriage."

In a sense, Kya and Armstrong did live together. But his family would've been surprised to know how often Kya would disappear for days. Some days she couldn't stand to be in her human form. Other days the sky and Buto called to her dragon spirit.

She always came back to him but in pieces. Kya was never whole when she wasn't in dragon form. Those nights, after being away, when she would return, they'd make love with so much passion Armstrong would forget how lonely he'd been without her.

Tonight was one of those nights. It was their anniversary, not that Kya cared about such milestones. Armstrong did, though. It had been thirteen years since she'd seen him in the alley outside of Knight Life Bar and sought him out in his apartment. Thirteen years of loving a dragon and five years of having the human Kya share his life.

He moved inside of her, and she felt so good. Kya always did. A year, that's how long it had taken before they consummated their relationship. The wait had nearly killed Armstrong, especially with the way Kya liked to rub against him in her sleep. But waiting had been for the best. When they finally took their relationship to the physical level, Kya had wanted him as much as he wanted her.

"I missed you," he whispered in her ear.

She turned her face to him and kissed Armstrong. Deep and long and with an erotic display of tongue. His dragon had mastered the art of kissing, of which Armstrong was the happy beneficiary.

"I missed you as well." She arched in his hungry embrace. "Touch me there again, diata."

She didn't tire easily and was rarely winded. Yet when they made love, he managed to leave her breathless and panting for more.

He touched her where she liked, and Kya moaned into his mouth. He desired nothing more than to taste her, and now that she understood what that entailed, he slid down her body with confidence.

Mouth first found breasts and kissed. Then engorged nipples and sucked. Lips pressed into her toned stomach, kissing then licking before dipping lower. Big hands spread thighs and nose nuzzled the V of hair there.

Kya sucked in a harsh breath, and Armstrong did it again. He wouldn't tease her. She didn't understand or appreciate the sensual power of delayed gratification. So he sank his tongue down, around, and in. Vanilla and honey, his dragon's signature flavor.

Delicious.

"Armstrong. Armstrong."

He loved the way she moaned his name. Kya had never been a loud or talkative lover. She didn't swear when she came or talk dirty. She didn't flirt and wasn't coy. She didn't fake her orgasms or give him platitudes about his sexual prowess.

She did none of those things, which made Kya the best lover Armstrong had ever had. His name. How he made her feel and what they did to each other when they made love was expressed in the way she said his name.

Velvety and sentimental.

Hips lifted and a hand came to his head. "Armstrong." She pushed her sex into his mouth, and he gladly accepted. Kya was wide open to him and the most human she would ever be. So close to her orgasm, with his tongue lapping at her clit, fingers driving in and out of her, Kya could be no more human than when on the verge of her release.

"Armstrong please." A soft plea.

He knew what she wanted, and he gave it to her. Closing his mouth around her clit, Armstrong sucked with a gentle tug. That was all it took for his dragon to explode into a rapturous release.

Seconds later, she pulled him to her and Armstrong sank into the warm wetness of his Kya.

CHAPTER NINE

"ARE YOU SURE?"

Armstrong had asked her that question five times. Kya refused to answer it again. Yes, she was sure. Yes, she'd been seen by a gynecologist. Yes, she'd gotten a second opinion.

Yes. Yes. Yes. Kya was certain she was pregnant.

She sat on the couch in the living room while Armstrong, still in his black Secret Service uniform, sans the bulletproof vest, stalked back and forth. She wished he would sit down or at least stay still. His agitation wasn't helping nor would it change their predicament. They'd taken precautions to prevent conception. Clearly, they hadn't been cautious enough.

Before they became intimate physically, Kya explained about dragon-human reproduction and Kesins. Armstrong assured her he would "take care of everything." In the weeks leading up to their first night together as lovers, Kya had learned much about human conception. Since neither of them knew how genetically human dragons became when they shifted, Armstrong was uncertain if female contraceptives would be effective or safe for Kya to use. When she'd given herself to him that first time, and every time afterward, Armstrong wore a condom.

Except, at least once, he did not. Kya's unplanned pregnancy was the result. The sad truth wasn't that the offspring was unwanted, despite the unexpectedness of the news. Kya and Armstrong wanted to share parenthood, desired nothing more than to create and raise a product of their love. But no offspring of their union could live among humans without revealing secrets of the Dracontias.

Armstrong dropped to his knees in front of Kya. If she were in dragon form, she would be able to smell his sadness and desperation. She didn't need her enhanced senses, however, because everything her diata felt was in the agonized eyes that met Kya's and in the hands that gripped hers with fierce possession.

"I should be happy. I want this. I want our child." He kissed her lips. "But I want you more. I can't lose you, Kya. I don't want to go back to living my life without you."

Kya didn't want that either. She'd known their relationship wouldn't last. She just never imagined it would end so soon. With a young dragon to care for, Kya wouldn't have time to spend with Armstrong. She couldn't leave their Kesin for days and weeks while she played human and courted her feelings for him.

"Don't smack me or get mad. There's another option, we should consider."

"What option?"

He squeezed her hands. "Sometimes, when a woman becomes pregnant and isn't ready for motherhood, she aborts the fetus. The father may want the same thing, although she's the one who decides because it's her body. Do you understand what I'm saying?"

"Abort," she said, repeating the word and thinking about its meaning in the context of what Armstrong had just said. "Are you suggesting I abort our young before it has a chance to be birthed?" Kya withdrew her hands from Armstrong. "You want me to deny life?"

"No, not want. Dammit, Kya, I want our baby. I want you both. But if you have the baby, you'll go away and take our child with you. If that happens, I won't have anything."

"I'm a healing dragon."

"I know."

"You don't. What you ask is not done. Every dragon, Afiya or Kesin, is like the stone in our skulls, unique and precious. We can live without our Dracontias stone, but the power of the stone is worthless if the dragon owner of the stone dies."

"What does that mean?"

Kya felt tears pooling, and she wiped them away. Too many uncontrolled emotions as a human and far too few ways to conceal all she felt. They should've been more cautious. This is what came of losing control of one's emotions, of being too human and less dragon.

She no more wanted to lose Armstrong than he did her. Over the years, Kya had adjusted to and adopted many human customs. But this, the aborting of her young, she couldn't do such a thing, not even for her love of Armstrong.

"It means the might of the Dracontias aren't our healing stones and magic. It's not our long lifespans and armored scales. What makes us powerful and a threat to humans is our unbreakable bond and unconditional love. We're unwavering in both. I'm a dragon, Armstrong. Abortion is not an option. I'm sorry."

For more than he would ever know. In all she'd explained, the implication was that she would forsake their love and him for the Dracontias. The pain and realization were there, in the eyes that lowered and the body that slumped to the floor.

She'd hurt him, and she'd hurt herself. If there were any way for them to be together as a family, Kya would do all within her Bloodstone

Dragon power to give them that life. Their Kesin couldn't stay in the land of humans, and her Armstrong couldn't live on Buto with dragons.

Their worlds would have to stay forever separate. They'd tried to bridge the divide. For a while, they'd fooled themselves into believing in miracles. But there was no miracle to be found, not even with all the magic on Buto and within the Dracontias.

"I'm sorry." Tears fell, and she couldn't stop them from falling. Kya dropped to the floor beside Armstrong and pulled him to her. He came, wrapping his arms around her waist and settling his head in the crook of her neck. "I'm sorry."

"I know. What am I going to do without you?"

She had no idea because she didn't know what she would do without him.

"I love you, Armstrong Knight. I have for a very long time."

A confession she'd pledged to never make because the repercussions for her heart would be too great. But a broken heart couldn't break twice, and hers had fractured the moment she'd learned of her pregnancy.

She hoped telling Armstrong how she felt would help alleviate the pain of the parting to come. It didn't. Her confession only served to deepen the wound.

"Will you at least stay until the baby arrives? You said Kesins are born human and will stay that way for a few months. If that's all the time I have, I want every second of it."

She lifted his chin, wiped the wetness from his cheeks and kissed him. He returned the kiss, feverish and forceful. Yanking Kya onto his lap, Armstrong deepened the kiss.

His hands tore at their clothing until they were naked and he overtop of Kya and driving into her. There was nothing gentle about their lovemaking, and she didn't need or want it to be. But it was passionate for all the love they shared and the loss they would have to endure.

Kya would miss Armstrong Knight. A part of her would even miss her human form and all the ways her diata made her feel like a woman.

She wrapped her legs around his waist, and he sank deeper. His moans of pleasure, low and gruff in her ear, were among her favorite sounds. There were others, such as his rich laughter, his soft snores and his grunts of release. She would miss those, too.

And his hands that held her while she slept.

The lips that kissed her good morning and goodnight.

The cold feet she kept warm in the winter.

The fingers that dug into her hips when they were intimate. And the heart that told her she was loved, no matter her form.

"I'll stay. Mmm, Armstrong. Do that again."

He did, his hips grinding just the way she liked.

"We're going to do this every day." A harsh bite to her neck. "Every day. You're mine, no matter where you are."

Kya was Armstrong's, his attempt at a claiming mark unnecessary.

"And you're mine."

"Damn right."

They exhausted themselves making love, starting and stopping and then beginning again. Filling up on memories, Kya knew, for the lonely days and nights ahead.

Armstrong had told her, several times, to take one day at a time, to not ruin the present by looking too far ahead to the future. For once, she saw the merit in those words. At most, Kya and Armstrong had fourteen months before she would have to return to Buto with their Kesin.

Not much time. Not much time at all.

After two weeks on the campaign trail with the president, Armstrong couldn't wait to see Kya and fall asleep in his bed with her by his side. The president's reelection bid was in full swing, which meant the commander-in-chief spent a lot of time away from the White House and DC. Which amounted to Armstrong also being away from home and Kya. They didn't have much time left, so he'd balked at the away assignment.

His supervisor had noted his displeasure and request for leave. Noted and then dismissed both. He and Kya spoke as often as they could, sometimes on the phone other times telepathically.

Her pregnancy hadn't been easy on the dragon. Morning sickness plagued her for the first and second trimesters. She'd lost weight instead of gained, which had Armstrong concerned. Kya had assured him she and the baby were fine. Now, with about a month to go, Armstrong was torn between wanting to see his child born and wishing Kya could stay pregnant forever.

Stupid, but each month that passed was one month closer to Armstrong losing his family. He'd watched Kya grow round and big with their child. He made every doctor's appointment he could, pampered Kya, and read to the baby. Armstrong strove to live a thousand lifetimes in the months left to them.

He'd taken dozens of pictures of Kya and her ever-growing stomach. Armstrong converted the small room he'd used as an office into a nursery and purchased bags full of baby clothing. He'd accepted donations for the baby from his siblings, and his colleagues had surprised him with a baby shower. They'd invited Kya and lavished gifts on the dragon, who had no idea how to respond beyond a polite smile and a genuine, "Thank you for your kindness."

So much fuss over a child who, in a few months, would be a baby dragon and unable to use any of the gifts meant for a human infant. Armstrong knew he hadn't faced his reality. Everything he'd done these past months mirrored the actions of a man who would soon become a father. He'd ignored Kya's soft, pleading eyes for him to accept the inevitable.

He couldn't. No more than Kya could shift. She'd been forced to forego her dragon form for the safety of their child. Her inability to transform into a dragon had left her uncharacteristically depressed. She slept too much during the day and spent the night hours on the roof staring at the sky. Armstrong never knew how she'd managed to climb onto the roof, particularly after she entered her final trimester.

With Kya unable to turn into a dragon, their home had become a revolving door of dragons in human form. He'd met all of Kya's siblings and her mother. They were as lovely as Kya and treated Armstrong like a member of the family. Their visits were irregular, and they didn't stay long. When they left, however, Kya was more like her normal self.

Her dragon family filled a void in her life he couldn't, no matter how hard he tried. They hugged and kissed her. They cuddled on the couch with Kya, stroking her hair and belly. They were, without a doubt, the most openly affectionate family he'd ever met. A dragon family, he finally saw. They would care for his child when Armstrong couldn't. Seeing them with Kya, loving and warm, he knew his baby dragon would be well taken care of by the Dracontias.

The thought should've brought him peace of mind, but it didn't. A father was supposed to provide love and security for his child. He could do neither. What he could do, however, was make sure his baby had a beautiful nursery to come home to, filled with toys, clothes and furniture from a father the baby would never know or remember.

It was a depressing thought that had Armstrong tossing his duffle bag onto the floor of the foyer and slamming the door closed. He didn't worry about disturbing Kya. He'd convinced her to stay with Isaiah and Nicole while he was away. She hadn't liked it, telling Armstrong, "I can take care of myself. I'm the Bloodstone Dragon."

She'd looked adorable, all round and indignant, he'd kissed her until her frown disappeared and she moaned, an arousing concession Armstrong had taken advantage of before he dropped her off with his family.

Standing in the middle of the foyer, Armstrong heard nothing in the empty house. It smelled of Kya. A sweet floral scent he would always associate with her. He stood there and listened. This would soon be his reality. An empty, quiet house. He wondered how long it would take after Kya left for her smell to disappear, too, denying Armstrong even that small connection to her.

A fist smashed into the wall. Again. Again. He ached to tear the whole goddamn house apart with his bare hands. What would it matter? Who would care after Kya and the baby were gone?

Armstrong raised his bloody fist to slam it into the wall again but stopped when the phone rang. He stared at his knuckles. They reminded him of the first time Kya had healed him. Back then, he'd had no idea how profoundly his life would change.

The ringing stopped, then started again. Who in the hell kept calling him? Couldn't a man wallow in self-pity without being interrupted? He guessed not because the person on the phone called him a third time.

Stalking into the living room, Armstrong picked up the phone. "What?"

"Armstrong, thank God you're home."

"Nicole. What's wrong? Did one of the girls fall off her bike again and get hurt?"

"No, nothing like that. It's—"

"Are those sirens in the background?"

"Yeah, listen, Isaiah's talking to the police."

"The police." Bloody knuckles forgotten, Armstrong's heart began to pound. "Nicole, I need you to tell me what's going on." She sounded like she'd been crying and her breaths were coming fast. "Calm down, and tell me why the police are there."

"You need to come over now. It's Kya. She's missing."

Armstrong didn't remember running out the house and leaving the door wide open. He didn't recall jumping into his car and speeding all the way to Isaiah's home. He had no memory of crashing his car into the curb in his haste to get out and find out what in the hell had happened to his Kya.

Armstrong remembered nothing but the screaming in his head. His voice telling him he was too late to save his family.

Kya wasn't missing. She didn't get up and leave. Kya never went anywhere without telling Armstrong. She may have been an independent dragon, but she was also a thoughtful one. Kya wasn't missing.

Kya had been taken.

Armstrong knew, with every bone in his body, the enemy he'd thought was out of their lives had returned. The 'how' of her disappearance confirmed what he'd already concluded.

The officers were gone, and he sat at the kitchen table with Isaiah and Nicole. They both looked terrible—Isaiah angry and worried, Nicole weepy and frightened.

"Are the girls okay?" he asked.

Nicole nodded, her face blotchy, eyes red and swollen. "I'm sorry. You asked us to watch Kya."

"This isn't your fault."

No, it was his. He'd kept the truth from Kya. Armstrong should've told her the real reason those five men had come to his home. If he had, she wouldn't be missing and in danger. Kya hadn't known there was a threat to her freedom, maybe even her life. His selfish need for his dragon was to blame. With his lie, he'd betrayed her, and now she was gone.

He'd given one of the officers the picture of Kya he kept in his wallet. He hadn't appreciated the sympathetic eyes and nod of the head. Armstrong had worked in law enforcement long enough to know what the officers thought about Kya's kidnapping.

They would search for her, do their due diligence, but they didn't expect to find her alive. If they found her at all.

The girls had told the officers Kya had been shot. She'd fallen to the ground and then four men had surrounded her. There was more to the story the girls hadn't told the police.

"I think those men followed Kya and the girls to the park," Isaiah said. "Michelle said she saw one of the men watching them as they played. She thought he was 'creepy,' so she told Kya."

Michelle was Nicole and Isaiah's oldest daughter. At nine, the girl was all long legs and bright smiles. She hadn't been smiling when she'd rushed into his arms, crying into his chest about, "Aunt Kya and those awful men."

"She said Kya gathered them up and headed for the park's exit. That's when the other three men appeared. They blocked their path." Isaiah pushed from the table, waves of fury wafting from his older brother. "They threatened my children, Armstrong. They cornered Kya and said they would hurt the girls if she didn't go with them."

Armstrong couldn't meet the hard, furious gaze of his brother. Not only had he put Kya in danger, but his actions could've also cost Isaiah his children.

Nicole's warm, small hand reached across the table, found his unharmed hand and held it. "Kya shoved them behind her, right before one of the men shot her in the shoulder. Michelle described it as a dart. There was no blood, and Kya didn't seem to be in pain. The man shot Kya two more times after that."

"They were hysterical when they got home." Isaiah slammed the palm of his hand on the countertop. "Do you know how they got home, Armstrong?"

He had a good idea what Kya had done. She loved and protected children. The men who'd taken her had to have known that, which was why they'd struck when they did. It also meant the men had Kya and Armstrong under surveillance and he'd never known.

Damn him.

"Fucking magic. Poof. One minute they were in the park, screaming their heads off because their aunt had been shot, and the next they were in the goddamn backyard. Scared the shit out of them."

"Kya sent the girls home. Bloodstone magic. Looks like red fog." On shaky legs, Armstrong stood. "The assholes knew they couldn't take her in a fair fight, so they used her affection for the girls to get close to her. The darts were probably some kind of animal tranquilizer."

"What the fuck are you talking about?"

"You know what I'm talking about."

He shoved the chair out of his way and approached his brother. If Isaiah wanted to take a swing at him, he damn well could do it while Armstrong was standing.

"The Knights may love Kya, but you also think she's strange, from the way she speaks to her eating habits and her mood swings. You've been too kind to say, especially since she's made me happy and is caring to everyone."

"The girls haven't been sick, not even a cold since Kya moved in with you." Nicole's hand came to her mouth, and she shook her head. "God, Armstrong, none of us have been sick. Momma Knight has never been healthier. It's as if decades have been taken from her."

"It's not possible." Isaiah slammed his palm against the countertop again. "Dammit, it's not possible."

"Kya is the Bloodstone Dragon. Gold and beautiful and taken because someone wants what isn't theirs to have."

Armstrong may have forgotten about the five men who'd come to his home, but he'd done his homework. With the help of a couple of FBI buddies, who'd he'd passed the driver's licenses along to, Armstrong had learned a lot about Captain Winston Rudolph and the other four men.

Ex-military. Special Operations. Hardcore. Professional soldiers who fought for money. That's who'd taken his dragon. Getting her back wouldn't be easy, especially since Armstrong's FBI friends hadn't been able to track down Rudolph's contractor.

When the first year had gone by without incident, and then the second, Armstrong had convinced himself that Rudolph and his men had either died on Kerguelen Island or their employer had lost interest and turned to other ventures.

It had never felt so painful to be wrong.

"It's true. Deep down, you know it makes sense. That's her secret. *Our* secret."

Nicole slumped in her chair. "Kya's a dragon. The gold dragon that heals children?"

"Yeah."

"I would say it's impossible, but I was standing in the kitchen looking out the sliding glass doors when Isabelle, Michelle and Jasmine appeared. Like you said, there was a fog. A lot of it. I didn't know what it was and didn't see the girls until they stumbled from the red cloud. I've seen her on television. Huge and gold, and never sticking around for applause or praise. That dragon is our Kya. I can see it, but it's hard to reconcile with the human Kya I know."

"If you want to punch me, Isaiah, do it now. I have important phone calls to make."

"Why in the hell would I punch you?"

"Because my secret endangered your children. Because I lied to everyone for years. Because I can't beat my own ass for what happened to Kya and our baby."

Two big arms yanked Armstrong forward. Isaiah hadn't hugged him since the day of their father's funeral. He'd cried like a baby then, thinking his life would never be the same without his dad. He'd been right. But he'd survived, thanks to Isaiah's strength.

He wished he could cry now. Armstrong damn sure felt like bawling. But crying wouldn't get Kya back and help his child.

"I can't fault you for falling in love and wanting to protect that love. I'd do damn near anything for Nicole. I wouldn't expect you to feel any differently about Kya."

"I can't get her back on my own." He backed away from his brother and toward the wall phone. "I have to break my promise to Kya. She may never forgive me, but I'll never forgive myself if I don't do everything I can to rescue her."

"Who are you going to call?" Nicole asked.

"The Director of the US Secret Service, who I hope will pass my story along to the president."

"That's a huge gamble," Isaiah said. "What if the government decides to only help you to get their hands on a shapeshifting dragon?"

He'd thought of that, which was why his second and third call would be to the *Washington Post* and *New York Times*.

"How many children do you think the Bloodstone Dragon has healed? More, what do you think will happen if all the dragons stopped healing humans because of Kya's kidnapping? Do you really think the president of the United States, who's running for reelection, would want to be responsible for driving the dragons away and for doing nothing to help the one dragon who's saved the lives of thousands of children?"

For the first time since arriving at his brother's home, Isaiah smiled. "From the poorest family to the rich and famous, the Bloodstone Dragon has touched the lives of many people. Even the Pope has praised her. I get it. You plan to out the dragons in order to turn the whole world into your ears and eyes."

"Someone, somewhere, must've seen or know something. Those mercs aren't amateurs, and their employer probably has enough money to buy silence and support. I need to leverage what I have. And what I have is a dragon story everyone will want, as well as the Bloodstone's Dragon humanitarian reputation. Those will be my sword and shield. It's all I have, Isaiah."

The Dracontias would likely kill him for revealing their secrets to the world. They could do whatever they wanted to Armstrong after he saved his Kya.

Nicole sat up straight in her chair, brown eyes full of worry. "What about Kya's family? I don't want to think about what they'll do once they learn Kya has been taken."

That was a problem for tomorrow. Tonight, he had a promise to break and a world to set on fire.

CHAPTER TEN

"DON'T WORRY ABOUT it, Rudolph." Dr. Kenneth Westmore slapped him on the shoulder. "Once this dies down, you'll be able to return home. They have nothing on you."

"They have my name, address, entire military history, and my face is plastered all over the goddamn television and newspapers. I have no idea what my wife thinks because I can't risk calling or going to see her."

"It's the price of success. Speaking of price, we wired your payment into your Swiss account this morning. You're a millionaire."

He said the last word in a sing-song voice, as if money replaced everything Rudolph lost and still had left to lose.

Dr. Westmore walked away from Rudolph and to the bank of televisions on the other side of the viewing room. Each screen displayed an image from one of the surveillance cameras inside the room adjacent to the one they were in. Miles underground and in a remote location, this labyrinth of reinforced steel was the equivalent of a panic room for the Circle of Drayke. More, the room Dr. Westmore watched with orgasmic pleasure had been designed for one purpose.

To contain the Golden Fleece.

"I can't believe it. The gold dragon. But not a dragon. A woman." The man, eyes bright with a lust that had nothing to do with the beautiful creature strapped to a gurney but with the sadistic anticipation of playing Victor Frankenstein, licked his lips. "I thought you and your team lied to hide your failure. A dragon that can turn into a human, ridiculous I thought." A long finger that hadn't known a day of hard labor ran across the unconscious face on the screen in front of him. "Beautiful. I can't wait to peek inside."

Thanks to Armstrong Knight and his pet dragon, Rudolph and his men had spent more than six months on an island he'd never heard of. They had no money and provisions and didn't speak the language. The dragon had dumped them in the middle of nowhere and left them for dead, which is what his wife had thought him. When he'd stumbled home, with no reasonable explanation for his long absence, his wife threatened to file for divorce if he ever did anything like that again. He supposed the million dollars could go toward lawyer's fees.

Rudolph hadn't lied to the Circle of Drayke. Who in the hell could make up a story like that? He'd been shocked when a red fog had surrounded him and his men, stealing his breath and crushing his bones. Powerful hands had clamped around arms, legs, and neck and squeezed. Even now, five years later, Rudolph could still hear the sound of his bones breaking.

He hadn't screamed or cried out. Not because he was military tough and didn't fear death, but because the woman in the middle of the fog wouldn't allow it. Her magic had controlled every molecule of his body, and her red eyes sparked dragon fire.

The next thing he remembered was waking. Cold, dazed, and smelling of shit. The dragon had won that day, reducing Rudolph to a terrified puppy who shits his load when scared. Today, Rudolph had reclaimed his manhood. If he'd had his way, he would've put a bullet between the dragon's eyes.

But no, the Circle of Drayke wanted him to bring the dragon in alive. Four years of waiting and watching had finally paid off. The Secret Service agent was a non-issue. A couple of his men could've taken care of the man. But the dragon, even in human form, was a force of freakish nature. So he'd bided his time.

Snipers, like Rudolph, were patient. There had been many missions where he'd go days hunkered down in the same spot, waiting for the perfect kill shot. The dragon's pregnancy turned out to be his perfect kill shot. Once one of his men noted the dragon's protruding stomach and increased frequency at the house she shared with Armstrong, Rudolph scented the opening he'd been waiting for.

He had to make sure, so the rotating team of men who'd observed the dragon's every movement was tasked with documenting everything. Their notes proved revealing, as did the notable absence of the gold healing dragon over North America.

Rudolph grinned now as he did then, wide and malicious. He had her. The dragon, knocked up by her human lover, disgusting, no longer shifted into her dragon form. He hadn't known if her pregnancy made her weaker, which meant he needed a plan that would put the dragon at a disadvantage and his men in the best possible position to take her down.

It had taken three tranquilizers meant to incapacitate a ten-thousand-pound adult male elephant to drop the dragon. They'd had to shoot her again halfway to their secret location. She'd begun to stir, red vapors hissing and snapping from her nose, mouth and ears. One tranquilizer to the neck got them through the rest of the flight.

"How human do you think that monstrosity inside her belly is?" Rudolph didn't get it. Sure, the dragon's human form was beyond beautiful. But she was still an animal for God's sake. "She looks ready to pop."

"She is. A month, maybe less."

"Well, tell you what. Whatever you're going to do to her, I suggest you do it before she gives birth." He banged the side of his fist against the closest reinforced wall. "I don't know how long we can keep her doped up and unconscious. Her body is fighting back, even when she's asleep. We must increase the dosage every time we shoot her up. If she gives birth, there's nothing stopping her from transforming back into her dragon form. If that happens, no amount of reinforced steel will keep her in and us protected."

Dr. Westmore straightened from where he'd been hunched over one of the television screens. "My problem. Yours is Armstrong Knight. He's making things difficult for us. We couldn't move her to another location even if we wanted to. Her human face is plastered all over the television and is in every major newspaper. He has public sympathy on his side, and the public wants their healing dragon found. Did you hear the president's last campaign speech?"

"Yeah. 'Dragons are our friends.'"

"Knight has managed, in a week, to galvanize the international community against us, even though he has no idea who we are. So far, the politicians we've paid off have kept silent. If Armstrong's one-man campaign continues, I'm uncertain if they'll stay that way."

"How much to take care of the agent?"

"Three hundred thousand. Make it look like a suicide. We want him silenced but not seen as a martyr."

"Consider Armstrong Knight already dead."

"Good. I'll let the others know." Dr. Westmore licked his lips again. His eyes had returned to the screen and the dragon. "One of the x-rays revealed a hexagonally shaped object below her frontal bone. I intend to find out what it is."

If anyone could, it was Dr. Westmore. The man wielded a scalpel like Rudolph did a gun. He left the mad doctor to his patient. Rudolph had a Secret Service agent to kill.

Two weeks and no kill shot. For that, he would have to get close to the man. Between the blackout curtains in every window of Knight's house to the Secret Service agents who followed him everywhere, Rudolph either couldn't get a clear shot or get away without being spotted and taken out if he did chance a bullet to the agent's head.

Then, there were the dragons. Jesus, he had no idea there were so many of those monsters. Dozens of them had slithered from their hiding holes and taken to the skies in search of the gold dragon. They were relentless in their hunt. When one disappeared, it was replaced by another.

Even now, as Rudolph pulled the baseball cap low over his forehead, shoulders hunched to his ears and keeping to the shadows, he could feel their heated presence patrolling DC.

The green dragon his men first encountered when they almost caught the gold dragon thirteen years ago had been Rudolph's biggest pain in the ass. Nightly, she'd perch her forty-foot body of menace on the roof of the agent's house.

He never saw her shift into a human during her vigil. She watched and waited. So had Rudolph. Come morning, she'd fly away just as the first shift of Secret Service agents arrived. Rudolph could almost respect Knight and the battle he waged to find his doomed dragon lover and to keep himself alive while his plan played out in the streets and in the news.

Worse than the predatory dragons were the enraged public. Knight had given the gold dragon a name and bestselling story. The stupid public loved nothing more than a good hero-villain tale. Kya, the Bloodstone Dragon. Children's Guardian Dragon. Diamond in the Sky.

The titles were endless and the reverence contagious. The men who'd helped Rudolph capture the dragon were in custody, thanks to anonymous tips. It would be a matter of time before a dragon-loving asshole spotted him and dropped a dime.

Which was why it had to be tonight. With the green dragon else-where and the last Secret Service shift gone for the night, Rudolph wouldn't find a better opening than this one. There was also no way he could make this kill appear anything other than what it would be. Mur-der. Westmore was a fool if he thought anyone, least of all Knight's boss, would believe the secret service agent, so broken up over the loss of his pregnant dragon, would take his life.

Nothing about the agent screamed suicide. Rudolph would end the man his way.

Pulling his powder coated stainless blade from his ankle sheath, Ru-dolph wedged the knife between a window and the lock. He'd slipped unnoticed around the back of the house. From this position, he wouldn't be seen from the street as he worked his blade back and forth. A line of thick shrubs separated Knight's backyard from his neighbor's. Lights were out next door and the house quiet.

Snap.

Rudolph smiled, held onto his blade as he pushed up the window and crawled inside. Television, couch, bookshelves and floor lamps, Knight's den. Rudolph remembered this room from the last time he was in the man's house. He'd committed every room to memory. From the looks of things, little had changed in the intervening years.

To the right of the den was a short hallway which led upstairs. Three bedrooms and a full bath. At the end of the hall and to the right was the master bedroom.

On silent booted feet, Rudolph climbed the stairs. He had a gun at his waist, but he still held the lethal blade in his right hand. The gun would be quicker and clean. He could stand in the doorway to the man's room, aim and shoot. The silencer would guarantee no one heard any-thing suspicious coming from the Knight residence.

But Rudolph didn't want quick. A slow and messy kill, that's what had him sneaking into Knight's home and creeping into his bedroom. He'd begin with removing the tongue that had incited the nation and then the world. Then he'd take the brown eyes that had stared into the cameras with a mix of sorrow, hope, and determination.

Finally, Rudolph would cut Armstrong Knight's heart out. How dare the man love a dragon more than he did his own kind. Maybe he'd even take the bloody organ back to the dragon so she'd see what he'd done to her pathetic human. Then again, after weeks with Dr. Westmore, Rudolph doubted if any part of the gold dragon remained.

Stepping inside the pitch-black room, Rudolph could make out nothing. As quietly as possible, he pulled his night vision glasses from a deep side pocket in his cargo pants. Slipping them on, he saw a lump in the bed. Covers up to shoulders, the man in the bed snored, unaware his life would soon end.

Rudolph crept forward. The carpet absorbed the little sound he made. Yes, after tonight it would be done. He could fly the hell away from DC and the stench of circling dragons. He'd find a country where he could lay low until the dragon's kidnapping and Armstrong's death were footnotes in people's memories. Soon enough, some other sensational news event would distract them and they would lose interest, forgetting all about Rudolph, Armstrong and the Bloodstone Dragon.

The handle of the blade felt good. It would feel that much better when he sank it into the sleeping man's body. Rearing up, then plunging down, he drove the blade into Knight's neck.

The metal shattered on impact.

Lights flickered on.

Rudolph held a broken knife pressed to the throat of a man. A man who wasn't Armstrong Knight.

Click.

Eyes flew up. Standing inside a closet that hadn't been opened a minute ago was the Secret Service agent. Dressed in jeans, T-shirt, and a bulletproof vest, he held a SIG Sauer P229 sidearm in his hand. The silver-and-black gun was pointed at Rudolph's head.

A clawed hand came up and circled his neck. In an effortless move, Rudolph was lifted off his feet and into the air when the man in the bed rose.

The dark-brown arm holding Rudolph rippled with muscles as did the massive neck that led to impossibly wide shoulders and a chiseled chest. The behemoth's other hand plucked the handgun off Rudolph's hip, the sound of crushed gunmetal loud in the quiet room. That same big hand rose to his face. Off came his night vision glasses, tossed to the floor and then smashed under the giant's foot.

The eight-foot man, eyes reddish-brown and narrowed to deadly slits, opened his mouth and roared. A wide snake tongue came out and smacked Rudolph across the face. Acidic saliva burned the skin where the wet tongue touched, and the mercenary screamed.

Knight stepped from the closet and lowered his weapon. "Meet the Aragonite Star Dragon." The Secret Service agent looked from Rudolph and to the immovable hand clutched around his neck. "I told him you would come. I didn't want to make it too easy for you or you would've suspected something. This is the thing, Winston Rudolph, we want to know who you work for and where we can find Kya."

Another acidic tongue slash to his face, over his nose and around his left eye. The skin melted, and Rudolph whimpered his pain.

"Let me tell you a secret. One I didn't reveal on the news. Very mature dragons, like Kya's parents and her two oldest siblings, can shift into whatever human form they wish. You get what I'm saying, asshole?"

Yeah, he did. Every time he thought he saw a different set of agents arrive at Knight's home they were, in truth, the same dragons in a different human form. He wondered how many times when he thought he had Knight in his sights if it was really the big beast choking the shit out of him.

"This is the thing, you're going to die. There's no way of getting around that. For taking Kya, I want to beat the hell out of you until you cry her location and wet your camouflage boxers. But I won't because the Aragonite Star Dragon gets the honors. So, this is where you stand. He can take you outside, turn into a really big gold dragon and devour you in one pitiful swallow, or…" Armstrong sat at the foot of the bed. "I just remembered, there's no or. That's how you'll die. He's going to eat you. Plain and simple."

"Ask again." The dragon's thunderous voice slammed into Rudolph.

"Where's our Bloodstone Dragon? Why did you take her? And who do you work for?"

Even if he wanted to, Rudolph barely had enough air to breathe no less answer Knight's snarled questions.

The Secret Service agent stood and walked up to where Rudolph hung from the dragon's debilitating grip. "Where's our Bloodstone Dragon? Why did you take her? And who do you work for?"

With a release of his meaty hand, the dragon dropped him to the floor. He scrambled backward until his back met a dresser. His face hurt like hell, and the last acidic lick had left him blind in his left eye. But he could breathe, which he did fast and hard.

"Do you have the information?"

"I do. The Circle of Drayke. They have my Kya underground, which explains my inability to scent and track her."

"Did you pick up anything else from his mind when I asked the questions?"

From his what? What kind of magic was this? How had the dragon plucked those details from his head?

"Don't look so shocked, Rudolph. Old dragons are special in ways you can't begin to imagine. But our human minds are predictable. You ask us a question, even one we have no intention of responding to, the answer comes unbidden to our minds. It's the way we are. There's no shame in being human."

The cold, smug gaze that had been on Rudolph switched to the dragon in human form. "Do you know where she is?"

"Yes, but he left her in vile hands."

Captain Winston Rudolph, throat bruised and sore, laughed. It came out more like a desperate cough, but he didn't care. He may be a dead man, but Knight and the Aragonite Star Dragon wouldn't reach the Golden Fleece in time to save her from Dr. Westmore.

So he laughed and laughed and laughed. Until he gurgled up blood, a gunshot wound to his stomach.

"You're going to pay for hurting my Kya."

Rudolph felt himself being dragged out of the master bedroom by Knight, down a flight of stairs, through a kitchen and into the backyard. He lay on his back, bleeding out and in excruciating pain. All overhead was black, not a star in the sky.

Except one. A bright gold star that got closer the faster he blinked and the louder he screamed.

The Aragonite Star Dragon, enormous teeth and—

Armstrong didn't look away when Kya's father consumed the screaming Rudolph. For what he feared had befallen Kya, the man deserved his fate.

You are a true diata, Armstrong Knight. I thank you for your courage and cunning.

Armstrong didn't deserve this magnificent dragon's gratitude. He'd taken too long to discover Kya's whereabouts. If she and his child lived, it would be a miracle. For two weeks, he'd sat on his roof, the way Kya used to do, and gave himself a migraine as he attempted to contact Ledisi. Kya's oldest sister was the only member of her family he'd seen often enough that he thought he might have a chance to link with telepathically.

When she'd first spoken in his mind, sounding so much like Kya, he'd nearly fallen from the ladder he'd been descending from the roof.

Gold-and-green forms filled the sky over Armstrong's house. He guessed the Aragonite Dragon had called his family. A metallic gold dragon with green flecks was all that was missing from the group of resplendent flying beasts.

A dragon family. He should've never gotten between Kya and the world she loved. A world that could protect her. He'd done his best. Loved his dragon the best way he knew how. But it hadn't been enough.

He waved at Kya's family and walked away. His part of the plan was done. The dragons would rescue Kya and kill whoever dared to stand in their way. They didn't need a useless human.

Where are you going, Kya's diata?

Armstrong halted at his back door and then turned around to see a huge golden tail leading from his feet and to the Aragonite Star Dragon, who watched him with reddish-brown eyes.

I take it you know how to climb upon and ride a dragon?

"Um, yeah. I mean, Kya showed me."

Then make haste, Armstrong Knight. I do not wish to keep the Bloodstone Dragon waiting any longer than she already has been.

Running back into the house to retrieve his gun, Armstrong wasted no time climbing onto the Aragonite Star Dragon.

The massive dragon took off, and Armstrong had never been so afraid and relieved in his life.

CHAPTER ELEVEN

ARMSTRONG HAD BEEN prepared to go through anyone to get to his dragon, including an army of mercenaries. In winding tunnels underneath London, Armstrong found nothing but trashed empty rooms. Whoever had been there had left in a real hurry.

"Kya."

Running from one room to the next, Armstrong yelled her name. Living quarters. Canteen. Bathrooms. He searched them all. Infirmary. He halted, and his stomach roiled at what he saw. OB/GYN Table, fetal monitor, exam lights, birthing bed.

How long had they planned this?

Oh, God. Dried blood stained the blue birthing bed. Swallowing hard, Armstrong approached the bed. Empty, like the underground compound of metal.

"Kya," he screamed again. Where in the hell was she? Had she given birth? If she had, where was their baby? "Kya." He bolted from the room. Frantic, he clutched his gun and ran down one corridor and then the next, Kya's name and his thudding feet the only sound on this level.

"Kya."

Gasira and Ledisi, in human form, searched the second level of the compound while Jahzara and her mate scoured the sewers that led from the compound and to the street miles above them. After reaching London, Kya's father had given each member of the search and rescue party their marching orders, including Armstrong.

There are ten responsible for tracking and kidnapping the Bloodstone Dragon, he'd said in everyone's mind. *See their images, know their faces.*

Pictures of ten men had begun to appear in Armstrong's mind as well as information about each man the Aragonite Star Dragon had stolen from Rudolph. The captain had known quite a lot about the group known as the Circle of Drayke. In less than three minutes, Armstrong and Kya's family of dragons knew it too. Names, addresses, and faces.

When most of Kya's sisters, six of them, had nodded at their father and flew away in different directions, Armstrong knew they were on a special mission. A search and destroy mission.

He'd left Kya's parents topside. They would guarantee their safety from the outside, making sure no mercenary got in or left the compound.

Armstrong had no idea how much was left on this level. He'd gone into every room he encountered. No soldiers for hire, no baby, and no Bloodstone Dragon.

Rushing down another sterile corridor, Armstrong skidded to a halt when he reached a closed door. Gunmetal, like all the others. This one, however, leaked blood from underneath.

Holding his weapon steady in his right hand, he wrenched the door open with his left. He'd found the guards he'd expected to battle. Inside the small room, bloodied, twisted bodies littered the floor. Broken guns lay at their side.

It smelled awful. The foul stench of blood and death clung to everything in the room, including the putrid frigid air. He didn't question what happened or who had been kept in this room. A gurney, wrecked and in a corner of the room on its side, straps ripped and sidebars crushed, did that for him.

"Kya," he whispered her name. This had been her cell, but she'd turned it into a room of horrors for her guards.

Holstering his sidearm, Armstrong stepped over and between dead bodies. There wasn't much room to maneuver or light to see by. Yet, he saw them. Footprints in the blood, smaller than the men's and with the curve and toe prints of bare feet.

The prints traveled away from the men and to the other side of the room. Lifting his head, Armstrong saw, for the first time, a one-way wall-mirror.

Shattered.

Two footprints ended at the base of the wall that connected this room to the one on the other side. Taking out his gun again, Armstrong led with his gun hand, sticking it through the opening before climbing up and jumping down.

Shards of glass crunched underneath rugged boots. More spacious than the cell the bastards had kept Kya in, this room and occupants had suffered the same fate. Dead bodies in military fatigues slouched in chairs, under tables, and over cracked monitor screens.

Less sticky, thick crimson but the same grisly fate.

On the floor, prone but with jasper green eyes open and staring at the ceiling amidst the corpses of her victims, was the most beautiful and wretched sight Armstrong had ever seen.

Dried blood under fingernails, on the bottom of feet and the center of her forehead, Kya lay sprawled on the aluminum floor. Dressed in a blue-and-white print hospital gown spotted with blood and torn in various places, Kya didn't stir when Armstrong called her name and approached.

With caution, he knelt beside Kya and waved his hands a few inches in front of her face. She didn't blink or otherwise acknowledge his presence.

Unbidden, his eyes traveled from her dull, lifeless face and to her stomach. Her childless stomach. Armstrong swore, low and pain-filled. He didn't bother to search the room. If their baby were there, Kya wouldn't be despondent.

Other than the blood, which was probably from the soldiers she'd killed, she didn't appear physically harmed. Although he had a terrible feeling about the blood on Kya's forehead and the crumpled X-rays on the metal table.

I found Kya. I'm bringing her out.

Lifting her into his arms, Armstrong held Kya close to him and fought the urge to curse and cry. Halfway up to street level, he encountered Gasira and Ledisi, who stared at Kya's boneless form and vacant eyes with the same fury and sadness eating him from the inside out.

"Is she hurt?" Armstrong asked, uncaring which of the healing dragons answered.

Gasira stepped forward, tall and muscular like his father. Except where the Aragonite Star Dragon was bald, Gasira's human form had shoulder-length dreadlocks. He laid his hands on the gown covering Kya's stomach.

"She's healed from the forced removal of her young one."

Armstrong shifted Kya upward, pressing her face to his chest and his lips to the crown of her head. It was either that or breaking down and swearing a stream of fruitless curses. The man who did this to her would pay.

Gasira's steady hand pushed Kya's riotous hair out of his way. He frowned at the blood on her forehead, lifted his eyes to Armstrong and then over his shoulder to his older sister.

"It's still there."

"Yes, I can see the magic within the Dracontias."

"What's still there?" Armstrong had no idea what the siblings were talking about.

Ledisi appeared by Kya's head, face set in granite, her voice like liquid steel. "Gasira saw recent evidence of an attempt at brain surgery. So do I." She found Kya's limp hand and held it with a tenderness he'd seen between the sisters many times before. "She was drugged, then operated on. Drugging us is the only way to get a dragon in a state where our Stone of Dracontias can be removed."

"What? You're saying someone tried to steal Kya's Bloodstone?" He remembered the X-rays in the room. Some of them had been of a skull.

"Yes, tried. But they didn't succeed. Even in human form, our craniums are not easily breached, which must happen if one is to claim our healing stone." Ledisi drew Kya's hand to her mouth and kissed it before placing the appendage on Kya's stomach next to her other hand. "She may have even awoken during the operation. We won't know unless she decides to speak of it."

From the way Kya curled against him, tears tumbling from the corners of her eyes as her sister spoke, Armstrong didn't think Kya would want to relay the horrors done to her in her prison and on the birthing bed.

The way Gasira watched Armstrong as he carried Kya through the maze and out onto a busy London street, he thought he might have to fight the man for his sister. He wouldn't win, but he'd be damned if he allowed anyone to take her from him again.

When the Aragonite Star Dragon and the Bluestone Dragon landed in the middle of the street, stopping traffic and drawing shocked and curious onlookers, Armstrong knew his time with Kya was at an end.

Her parents lowered their massive heads to Kya and blew wisps of magic on her from their noses. She blinked wet eyes but didn't otherwise move.

Kya's mother blew again, and a blue fog of magic floated from her nose and to Armstrong and his dragon. It encircled them, lifting Armstrong off his feet and into the air. Miles of open, quiet sky stretched everywhere as the fog carried him along.

The dragons flanked them, with the Aragonite Star Dragon, to Armstrong's surprise, flying the closest to him, his concerned father's eyes on his now sleeping daughter.

At some point, Armstrong must've dozed as well because when he stirred, the fog was gone. He still held Kya, but they were both on the back of the gold dragon. His eyes widened when he saw acres of plush land and herds of wild elephants.

Welcome to Buto, Kya's diata. As the mate to the Bloodstone Dragon, you may also consider this your home and the Dracontias your family.

———◦———

Kya awoke by slow, painful degrees. Her body hurt nowhere except her heart, which had her opening her mouth and roaring her grief and loss. It wasn't until then she realized she was in dragon form. Months she'd yearned for the familiar feel of smooth scales, fire in her belly, and claws cutting through the night sky.

She roared again. Her mind assaulted by one horrible memory after another.

"Kya."

She kept roaring, unable to express her sorrow in tears as she'd done when she was weak and vulnerable in her human form.

"Kya, please. I'm here. You're safe now."

Two hands touched her. On the side of her body and in the same location where her Kesin once dwelled. Whole and safe and not yet ready to be born.

In a blind fury, she flipped from her side and onto her feet, strengthening her scales and knocking the human who dared to touch her on his back. Hissing, she opened her mouth. No human would ever lay hands upon her again. She would kill them first rather than let herself become a prisoner again.

"No, Kya, it's me. Armstrong."

She knew that name. That voice. But it couldn't be. Armstrong was... Kya raised her head and looked around. The Eshe Forest. Sights and sounds came back to her. The chirping of birds in the trees above her head. A small family of elephants clomping through the rolling grassland downwind and to her right. The scent of damp earth and fallen leaves. The thudding heart and sweat of the human she was about to devour.

Kya backed away. This was Buto, and the haggard man with days' worth of stubble was Armstrong Knight.

He stayed on the forest floor but rose to a seated position. Minutes passed and he said nothing, which was unlike him.

Kya also remained quiet. She didn't know what to say to him or how to explain her powerlessness to save their offspring. Kya had tried to fight against the drug the humans kept inserting into her body. But each dose had left her drained and unable to focus her magic.

For much of her time in the room, she hadn't been fully unconscious, including when the man in the white coat drilled into her head. He swore when the fifth saw broke. After that, Kya recalled little until she'd awakened again, her baby and the doctor gone.

In her rage, she'd slaughtered every human who'd entered her prison room. Then scented the ones on the other side of the wall. Smashing through the window, she'd gone after those men as well, breaking backs and necks. Collapsing to the cold, metal floor, Kya had waited for the pain in her ravaged soul to cease.

As she settled onto the ground, her stomach on the crisp leaves, Kya realized the pain would never go away. She also admitted another truth to herself.

Armstrong had lied to her. Worse, the weak, needy human part of Kya had known the men who'd attacked Armstrong in his home had been there for her. The same kind of men who'd tried to capture her when she'd first left Buto as the Bloodstone Dragon, the smallest of the Dracontias.

She'd known, or rather she'd suspected the truth. But love, desire, and youth made for a lethal blend of ignorance and delusion.

Humans don't belong on Buto.

"Your father brought me here. Said this was my home. You've been asleep for two days. I was worried when you shifted but didn't wake up. How are you feeling?"

Armstrong no longer had a right to her heart and feelings, no more than he belonged on Buto and with Kya.

You have a gift indeed, if you've softened the heart of the Aragonite Star Dragon.

"Yours is the only dragon's heart I care about. I'm sorry for lying to you. I know it's too little too late and doesn't change a damn thing. But I am sorry. I had no idea any of this would happen."

His hand rose as if he could reach out and touch Kya. His arm was too short and Kya too far away. As if realizing the same, he dropped his arm back to his side.

"I'm sorry. About the kidnapping. About the torture. About our baby. I'm sorry for it all." He stood, leaves falling from him as he rose. "If you're wondering, your sisters took care of eight of the ten men who've been hunting you. The doctor, Kenneth Westmore, and Hugh Cafferty, a businessman, are still unaccounted for. Your father wants them dead, but now that you're safe and back where you belong, he doesn't seem as intent on finding them. I can tell by your silence and distance that you don't want me here. It hurts like hell, but I understand. If you don't believe anything else, know that I love you with all my heart. I'll spend the rest of my days hunting Westmore and Cafferty and seeking your forgiveness."

Kya said nothing when Ledisi landed behind Armstrong. He must've called her because she didn't. When had he learned to communicate with a dragon other than Kya? It didn't matter. She was grateful for her sister's appearance. Not only did she not think, in her current state, she'd make the trek from Buto to DC, Kya knew she couldn't have Armstrong touch her without remembering the doctor's unkind hands. An unfair psychological overlay but one she couldn't disentangle from her mind.

"I could return your diata tomorrow or the next day. You've only just awakened. He's waited to speak with you."

"He spoke, and I listened."

"You had nothing to say?"

"I had too much to say, which is why I said nothing. He doesn't' deserve my hateful tongue and bitter heart. I'm raw, and he's here when those who hurt me and took my Kesin are not. It would be all too easy to lash out at him. Take the human home, Ledisi, and never bring him back."

With skill, Armstrong climbed onto Ledisi. His dark eyes remained on hers, and he smelled of guilt, sadness and love.

"I'm sorry, Kya."

Ledisi lifted a few feet off the ground and waited.

"Are you sure? We have human food and shelter for him. He'll be comfortable if you wish to extend his stay."

"I wish nothing of the sort. Take him home. The Knights will be worried."

Before Armstrong or Ledisi could utter another word, Kya ran into the brush and away from the human she loved and the heart that ached for all she lost and could never have.

CHAPTER TWELVE

"THIS ISN'T RIGHT." The Cafferty family owned many businesses and even more homes around the world, including a medieval castle in southern Ireland. Thus, the past eight years had proven more an inconvenience than uncomfortable.

"So you've said, and so I'm tired of hearing."

Hugh followed Kenneth as the tall man stalked down the dark, winding steps. Lit wall torches provided light, although the Caffertys had electricity added to the castle decades ago. Yet Dr. Kenneth Westmore, theatrical in everything he did, insisted on the torches, claiming they added "historical ambiance" and aided his "scientific muse."

Hugh had met Kenneth their freshman year at Harvard. Four years later, Hugh had moved onto Harvard Business School and Kenneth to the medical school. Quiet, intelligent, and intense, that's what Hugh thought of Kenneth when they were eighteen and didn't know a damn thing about the world but had huge dreams to make it theirs.

Thirty years later, Kenneth was still quiet, intelligent and intense. But their dreams, which they'd founded the Circle of Drayke on, were larger than they'd ever imagined. Every day, since embarking on their dragon hunt, Kenneth reminded Hugh of all they could achieve if they were willing to push the boundaries of science and morality.

After nearly a decade, Hugh hadn't gotten used to the cold of the dungeon and the forbidding hardness of the stoned walls and floors. No one entered this area of the castle except the two of them. The servants knew to stay away and to ignore the sounds that emanated from its depths.

Five brass dungeon master keys hung from a brass ring. The various keys, ranging from two to six inches in length, opened all the doors on this level, including the one Hugh and Kenneth now stood in front of. Unhooking the ring from his belt, Kenneth inserted the largest key, turned it and unlocked the door.

As old as the prison and castle were, the heavy door slid back without a sound. The quiet was an improvement over the crying and roaring.

The men stepped inside. Quiet, intelligent, and intense. Kenneth Westmore, MD, was still all three. As Hugh took in the barren cell and the pitiful creature in the corner, a heavy-duty shackle around his thin neck and the other end of the chain drilled into the stone wall behind him, Hugh added another descriptor to how he thought of the man.

Heartless.

Naked and skin a dull shade of brown from lack of sunlight, hair coarse, thick, and wild, eyes the color of a ruby, the creature watched, with a caged humanity, the men as they entered and Hugh closed the dungeon door behind them.

In the early days and when they'd first come to this castle, the creature had been a novelty and Kenneth's enthusiasm infectious. Neither had cared about the loss of the other members of the Circle of Drayke. They'd found the group, so it made sense they would be the sole survivors.

The red gem taken from the skull of the infant had Hugh throwing up. He thought the baby would die. To his amazement, he hadn't. Now, as he observed the crouched boy, frightened yet defiant in his captivity, Hugh wished he'd succumbed to Kenneth's experiments years ago.

Yet he always healed and continued to grow, displaying some of his mother's strength but none of her magical abilities. Days like today when the dragon was in human form, rare though they were, Hugh found it impossible to lie to himself. Inside the red-and-yellow dragon, left to rot in this cell until Kenneth wanted another blood sample, was a little boy of eight.

The abominations Kenneth created, from the hybrid blood and the stone, were locked in the other cells. Unlike this creature, who displayed intelligence and a range of emotions, the others did not. They roared and raged and, when taken out of their cells to roam the grounds of the sprawling estate, savaged and killed. Hugh had lost many good servants on those nights.

He'd also turned a blind eye when Kenneth lured men and women to the castle with promises of work and money. Prostitutes. Runaways. Criminals. Hugh had no idea where Kenneth found them all, but many came and none ever left.

His so-called dragon serum had yet to work the way Kenneth thought it should. But he had the young dragon's gemstone, which, even Hugh could sense, contained magical properties. Between the gem and the hybrid dragon's blood, Dr. Westmore had discovered how to transform a human into a dragon.

Far from perfect, the serum didn't react well with a human's brain, corrupting their higher brain functions and altering their psychological make-up, traits, and response styles. After the injection of the serum and the human to dragon transformation, what was left was a ferocious beast controlled by a savage human with a medical degree.

"We should put the boy out of his misery."

"I told you when he almost died as a baby, the gemstone and the hybrid are linked. The closer he drew to death, the weaker the stone pulsed magic and the lighter it became, a pale pink as opposed to a vibrant red. But when the boy's health improved so did the strength of the stone. His DNA can unlock the answers to slow aging and renewed health."

"Could, not can. It's theoretical. It's been a theory for over twenty years." Hugh pointed to the gray in Kenneth's hair then to the gray in his own beard. "We haven't gotten younger and this endless experiment is expensive. Maybe we should think about cutting our losses and moving on."

"No, we're too close. *I'm* too close."

"Has it ever occurred to you a dragon stone from a hybrid dragon will never yield the results we want? When we started the Circle of Drayke, the goal was to capture a real dragon." His gaze shifted to the boy who still watched them with far too much comprehension for Kenneth's comfort. "The boy may spend most of his time in dragon form, but he isn't a real dragon. Not like his mother."

They shouldn't have this conversation in front of the boy. For whatever reason Kenneth dragged Hugh down to the dungeon and inside the hybrid's cell, it could wait for another day.

Although he knew the dragon didn't have the strength to break the chains and do whatever was percolating behind his red eyes, Hugh's gaze never left his as he backed up and waited for Kenneth to open the door. Once ajar, he slipped out after Kenneth and waited for the man to lock the cell door.

The doctor may not want to kill the hybrid, but that didn't mean Hugh had to play witness to his madness. Until he solved the serum issue, he would keep to the upper levels of the castle and the hell away from the dungeon of horrors.

"Are you suggesting we begin hunting dragons again? We barely escaped our last encounter with them."

Hugh looked down the hall leading to the steps that would take him upstairs and away from the stench of failed experiments and lethal, mind-controlled dragons.

"What I'm suggesting, Kenneth, is that we use those monsters you created to draw the gold dragon out."

"Why in the hell would she care?"

"For a genius, you miss the obvious. You stole her baby. She probably thinks he's dead. I may not know as much about dragons as you do, but I remember every report from Captain Rudolph. Dragons have amazing senses. If you send those monstrosities to the North American cities she most frequents, you won't have to worry about finding her because she'll find them."

Kenneth laughed like the young, ambitious man he'd once been. In many ways, he was as bloodthirsty and depraved as the dragons he'd created. But he was still the smartest man Hugh Cafferty had ever met.

"They can fly now. Have I told you that?"

"No, but it'll make getting them to North America easier."

"The last time I had her, I couldn't break through her skull and that was when she was in human form."

"You're creative enough to figure something out. You only said the dragon must be alive for the stone to maintain its power. Alive and being in good health are entirely different states of existence. Without her tail or legs, she won't die. This dungeon is a fortress built to withstand most any siege. It will hold a disabled and weakened dragon."

"My dragons are smaller than the Bloodstone Dragon and nowhere near as powerful." Another laugh, giddy and with a trace of madness. "That means I'll have to make more. Many, many more."

———◦———

Kya never expected to find herself back there. If this weren't an emergency, she would've waited for Armstrong to return home. Perhaps that was the better option. She hadn't seen him since the day she'd asked Ledisi to return him to the Knights. To be more accurate, they hadn't spoken since that day. Two years after her kidnapping, she'd return to the land of humans and the healing of children. During her weak moments, she'd fly to the home she once shared with Armstrong. He looked well, although the exuberance that once radiated through him had dimmed.

He'd suffered in a way Kya hadn't known, hadn't wanted to know. Observing him, not at all the man she remembered, hurt a part of Kya she thought no longer existed. She didn't want to still love Armstrong Knight, yet she did. Despite the awful ending to their love story, Armstrong was an honorable man and would've made a wonderful father.

The door to Isaiah and Nicole's home swung open. Wide-eyed, mouth open, Armstrong stood there, silent and appraising.

You act as if you've never seen a dragon. Do close your mouth, Knight, before a fly decides to take up residence.

He closed his mouth and the door, which didn't prevent his family from peering at Kya from the windows. The human part of the Bloodstone Dragon desired nothing more than to transform into the human Kya the Knights knew and befriended. As much as she'd remembered her times with Armstrong, Kya also replayed happy memories of being a member of the Knight family.

Like her feelings for Armstrong, her love for his family hadn't diminished with her absence from their lives.

"I can't believe you're here." With quick, long strides, Armstrong closed the distance between them. "And in the middle of the day. Everyone is staring."

Yes, well, that was another reason she should've waited to seek him out. The Knights attended church on Sundays, although Kya never did when she lived with Armstrong. While his work schedule hadn't allowed Armstrong to attend as often as his mother would've liked, he attended when he could.

Of all that could've changed in the eight years they were apart, Kya knew the Knights Sunday morning church ritual followed by brunch at Armstrong's older brother's home had not. One of the faces in the upstairs window was Armstrong's mother, who waved at Kya with an enthusiasm she hadn't expected.

In turn, Kya nodded, then sent a wisp of healing magic through the air, under the windowsill and into the nostrils of Mrs. Knight. In a few seconds, her rheumatoid arthritis would be no more.

"You've gotten bigger. I even think you're more gold than before."

She had grown, but not by much. Of the adult dragons, Kya was still the smallest of the Dracontias.

I'm certain you and Father are the only two who've noticed the additional gold. He likes to think himself dominant, but Mother has left her green mark on most of their offspring. One male and one gold dragon out of eight, Father's claim to dominance isn't supported by the evidence.

She thought Armstrong would laugh. Kya had stated her father's hubris in such a way as to produce that desired result. She felt awkward and unsure, and it had nothing to do with the growing crowd of people.

Instead of laughing, Armstrong stepped closer to her, neck craned back and eyes lifted. "So beautiful. Seeing you on television has never done you justice. The Aragonite Star Dragon doesn't need more than one gold dragon. He has you, which is enough for any male, dragon or human."

She'd forgotten how easily Armstrong's words and earnest eyes could melt her heart and resolve.

Will you fly with me? There is much we need to discuss.

"The Kesins?"

Yes.

"I saw them on the news. From what I've read, they attacked you."

They had, three times in the last six months.

"You told me Kesins couldn't fly. That they had no Dracontias stone or magic."

That's what we need to discuss, but I don't wish to do it here.

"I don't suppose you'd be willing to return to our, I mean my house and have our talk there?"

Kya hadn't shifted into her human form since before her pregnancy. She may no longer harbor animosity toward humans over what happened to her, but that didn't mean Kya would ever again make herself vulnerable by taking on their form.

She glanced at Isaiah and Nicole's house again. The Knights were no longer at the windows watching them, but Kya could hear their chatter inside. Kya's unexpected arrival was on everyone's tongue, especially the girls, who hadn't seen Kya since that fateful day eight years ago. She'd protected them as best she could before the drug made her insensible and weak. It pleased her to see and hear how well they'd grown. Like all the Knights, Kya missed the children.

Not giving herself time to reconsider, Kya expelled a burst of Bloodstone magic. Her arrival had already caused a scene, why not give the neighbors even more to gossip about? Inside her fog of magic, Kya let the shift wash over her. The transformation was like peeling back the layers of her scales. Deep within her dragon body slept her human form.

With the touch of magic, the human Kya stirred from her slumber. She stretched and yawned within the dragon's protective body, her mind and form slow to process the command. Dusting off the last tendrils of confusion, the human knelt within the belly of the beast, arms stretched out to her sides and palms pressed against the dragon's body.

As the human Kya accepted the Bloodstone magic and the dragon Kya relinquished her dominance, the twin wills became one. The shift seamless and mutually accepted. The human Kya absorbed the Bloodstone Dragon, shifting her frame of reference from outside-in.

When the red fog evaporated, a fully formed and dressed Kya stood before a smiling Armstrong. The Bloodstone Dragon was now submissive to the human Kya dominant. Curling in a ball, she felt the dragon relax and fall asleep.

"You're still as beautiful as ever." Armstrong appeared as if he would embrace Kya when he stepped closer and began to lift his arms. Midway, his arms stopped then lowered and Armstrong stepped back. "Sorry, old habits die hard. You haven't aged a day in eight years."

She had, of course. But eight years to a human didn't equate to the same time for dragons.

"It's been twenty-one years since the first time we met. I was twenty-five and thought I knew more than I did. Now, I'm forty-six and realize I still have a lot to learn. But you, Kya, for a dragon you're still so young. Although, in many ways, you were always wiser than your years."

The temptation to lapse into their once comfortable conversations was strong. She'd forgotten how enjoyable speaking with Armstrong could be, particularly when he challenged her with his wisdom and insight. She'd forgotten because she refused to think of him and their time together. The tactic denied Kya the years of happiness they shared, but she couldn't have those memories without the horrible ones that marked the end of their relationship.

She wasn't there to discuss the changes in their lives, despite how much her new revelation would indeed alter much between them.

In silence, Armstrong led her to the front porch. They sat in the two wicker chairs facing each other, Kya's back to the house. Her frontal placement provided her with a full view of the street and sky. Until he'd given Kya that chair, she hadn't realized how unsafe she would've felt if her back was to the street and people. But sensitive, intuitive Armstrong had known how important it was for Kya, after what had happened to her, to feel in control.

"Not that I'm unhappy to see you or that you need a reason to drop by, but I know this isn't a social call. What does your visit have to do with those strange Kesins?"

Where to begin? Well, there was only one way to say it, so Kya did, without preamble.

"I have reason to believe our Kesin is alive."

She thought her words would shock Armstrong, but he only cast his eyes downward and shook his head.

"I always wondered. I even prayed. Then I thought what it would mean for our child to be alive without our love and protection. My thoughts were the stuff of nightmares because I knew if our baby survived, the child would be in merciless hands." Soulful dark-brown eyes rose. "Is that what you're telling me? Our child has been with Dr. Westmore all this time?"

Kya didn't know for sure, although it's what she thought and why she sought out Armstrong.

"You're right, Kesins cannot fly or possess a healing stone. Yet, I've fought, these past few months, many who can take to the air. They attack without true strategy and are wild and vicious in a way that Kesins are not. They smell wrong. They are Kesins to the eye only. The same way I'm human to the eye only. But this isn't my true form, and the same is true for those Kesins."

"I don't understand. How can there be dragons who look like Kesins but aren't? And where does our child fit in?"

Taking a pointless deep breath, Kya explained.

"Every creature in nature has a unique scent, Armstrong, including the two of us. I know your distinctive smell as well as I know my own and every member of my family."

"It took us so long to find you because no Dracontias, not even your parents, could detect your scent. Your father said it was because you were underground."

Kya had no idea whether the men who'd taken her to that awful place had known how well they'd selected her prison. If she'd been above ground and no dirt and metal to buffer her scent, her parents, no matter the distance, would've been able to track their offspring.

"I smelled traces of us on the Kesins."

He slid to the end of his chair. "You what?"

"Traces of us and a scent I'd never smelled before. But the smell was similar to ours."

"How is that possible?"

"It's only possible if our young lives and dragon blood is being used to recreate Kesins."

"That's insane."

"That human doctor who tried to steal my healing stone was insane."

"You think that's why he took our baby? That he hoped our child would have a healing stone?"

He left unsaid what they were both thinking about how the human would've retrieved the stone. But the anger that flickered in his eyes said it all.

"I've never known a Kesin to be born with a Dracontias stone or magical abilities."

"Perhaps that's only the case because there are so few Kesins born. You told me yourself, dragon-human matings are rare. Or maybe our DNA, when combined, is so amazing that we defy the norm."

"Defy the norm?" Kya couldn't help herself, she smiled.

"Yeah. I don't know how and I don't care. The bottom line, based on what you've said, is that our child is alive and at the mercy of Westmore, who I will kill. And that the asshole has not only taken our child's Dracontias stone but also used it somehow to create fake Kesins who can fly and have been attacking you."

"That's an accurate summary."

"You do realize that fool sent those fake Kesins because he still wants your Bloodstone?"

"I do."

"What do you want to do about it? How can I help?"

"I believed you when you said you would do all in your power to track down the men who were responsible for my kidnapping."

Armstrong jumped to his feet. "I have every bit of information I was able to scrounge up on the Westmores and Caffertys. File cabinets and floppy discs. Anything public on those families, I have it back at the house." He yanked Kya from her chair and hugged her tight. "Thank you for coming to me. Thank you for a chance at redemption."

Kya couldn't bring herself to return Armstrong's embrace, but she also couldn't force herself to withdraw from his hold. After so many years, being in his arms again felt perfect and all too right.

"We're going to bring our child home, Kya. I promise you, I won't let the two of you down again."

He hadn't let her down the first time. They'd both made mistakes. Kya may not have developed at the same rate as Armstrong, but she wasn't the same naïve and arrogant Bloodstone Dragon she'd been all those years ago. Heartache and loss had a way of forging the strongest of psychological swords—hardness, balance, strength, and flexibility.

As if realizing he held her too long and without her permission, Armstrong released Kya and stepped back with a soft, "Sorry."

"It's fine. How much time do you require to review your records?"

"I'll begin with the list of homes. For the Cafferty family, it's quite a few of them if my memory is right. But not all of them would be suitable to hold and hide Kesins. From what you've said, Westmore probably has many of them, which means he must have a place big enough for the dragons and far enough away from people that no one will see or hear them. My lists aren't exhaustive, though. It'll only take me a few hours to go through the documents. If nothing jumps out, I may need a few days to add to my database."

"Remote, large, and with an underground holding."

"My search criteria. Yeah, that's what I'll look for. In the meantime, make yourself more visible and see if you can't attract the Kesins."

"They're puppets. They won't lead us back to the human doctor if captured. I use my magic to salvage the ones I can. Unfortunately, most resist and die."

They were victims, just as Kya had been and just as her Kesin still was. She may not be able to return their humanity, but she could give them a peaceful death.

The front door opened, and Kya wasn't surprised to see Armstrong's mother, one hand on her hip, the other on the door.

"I hope you weren't planning on flying away without coming in and saying hello to everyone."

Kya had planned on doing just that. Rude, she knew, but the other option was an emotional quagmire she wasn't ready to tackle.

Mrs. Knight opened her arms. "Come here, Kya, and give this old woman a hug."

Unable to do anything other than submit, Kya moved to embrace the older human who smelled of myrrh.

"Oh, my sweet child, we Knights have missed you."

"I'm sorry."

"Sorry for what? For needing time to heal?"

"For lying. For being a coward."

"All nonsense." Mrs. Knight held Kya's face between her warm hands, lowered her forehead to her mouth and kissed. "I prayed for your safe return when you were taken. And I prayed you would, when the time was right, find your way back to your human family."

Her human family? She'd thought she lost this human connection with the dissolution of her relationship with Armstrong.

"Will you come in? Spend time with the family?"

Kya shouldn't. Self-preservation told her to reject the invitation and return to Buto until Armstrong contacted her with a location. But she found herself allowing Mrs. Knight to pull her into the house and close the door behind them.

In an instant, Kya was flooded with hugs, kisses and questions. Overwhelmed by so many Knights talking at once, she nearly missed when Armstrong, keys in hand, said, "I'm going home to check my files. I'll call when I have something."

CHAPTER THIRTEEN

"*I COULD'VE FLOWN* on your back.*"

"True, but I would've had to fly lower and at a slow pace. The flight to Ireland would've been long and uncomfortable."

"Ten hours and one stop are long."

"Yes. Would you rather have spent that time on a dragon's back with magical binds wrapped around your body?"

Armstrong peered out the window. He'd made sure to get a window seat so he could watch Kya. The dragon flew beside the plane, which made no damn sense. He'd flown with the Aragonite Star Dragon to London. He considered mentioning that fact to Kya when he remembered her father had encased him inside some mystical bubble during the flight that had permitted the dragon to fly at an accelerated speed, reaching Great Britain in record time. Armstrong had also fallen asleep on the flight from London to Buto.

He didn't like Kya had a point. Armstrong never minded her being right, so that wasn't his issue. His problem was that Kya was very good at putting distance between them, both physically and emotionally.

Once he'd begun his search, locating the files on homes owned by the Westmores and Caffertys, it hadn't taken Armstrong long to narrow the list down to one obvious location. How rich did a family have to be to own a goddamn castle? The lower walls that would become the Cafferty Castle were laid in 1320. He'd wanted to laugh as much as he wanted to shoot Westmore and Cafferty when he held a printed copy of a picture taken of the castle. Armstrong even remembered when he'd added the image to the manila folder, thinking power and privilege rarely resulted in good, upright behavior. All too often, entitlement bred a sense of immunity to the societal and legal limitations of the average person.

When he'd stared at the picture of the castle, the irony of dragon stories, medieval warriors and castles weren't lost on him. He'd known, with the same bone-deep certainty he'd always love Kya, they would find their stolen child at Cafferty Castle.

By the time he'd returned to his brother's home, Kya had appeared nothing short of a woman who'd survived a hurricane. Besides his mother and Isaiah's family, his sisters and their husbands and children were also there. Kya may have possessed a photographic memory, but dragons didn't track day, months and years the way humans did. So she wouldn't have known her reentry into his life coincided with Helen Knight's seventy-seventh birthday. His mother, a woman of deep faith, had viewed Kya's presence as a "sign from God."

As Armstrong watched Kya and thought about the great possibility of finding a child he'd considered lost to him, he couldn't help but agree with his mother. What he'd yet to figure out was what kind of sign from God it was.

"Do you have my guns?"

He knew she did. They'd argued about those too, with Armstrong claiming he needed to ride on her back because he wouldn't be allowed to carry firearms onto the plane. Kya, in dragon form, had taken one look at the arsenal of weapons he had in his trunk, snorted, and then said something about her being the Bloodstone Dragon and him not needing guns.

He'd disagreed.

"Why do you insist on asking such annoying questions? You insult us both when you do."

"That was the compromise. I'd take a plane, and you'd carry my guns."

"You know I have your weapons, Knight. Perhaps you should ponder the irony of your name and our intended location."

"I have, that's why I want my guns."

"A sword and shield make more sense."

"I'm a modern knight. Guns are better."

"Guns will not kill a crazed Kesin."

"I know. But bullets will do the job just fine for a human."

Kya's head turned to him. Green jasper eyes with slashes of red took him in.

"True."

For the rest of the flight, they didn't speak. He'd once spared the life of Rudolph and the men under his command. It felt like the right decision at the time, and perhaps it was. After all that had happened, though, Armstrong found it difficult to not think of that choice as a mistake.

As a Secret Service Agent, he'd never killed anyone, for which he'd been grateful. Now, as a father hellbent on rescuing his child and finally stopping the threat to his family, Armstrong was prepared to put an end to Hugh Cafferty and Dr. Kenneth Westmore.

"What do you hear and smell?"

From this height and at night, Armstrong couldn't see much. After landing, he'd made it to his hotel and checked in. Despite wanting to set out right away for the castle, he'd agreed with Kya. After a long flight, he wasn't at his best. He needed a decent meal and rest. While he'd slept, Kya had flown out to the castle and did a bit of reconnaissance.

Now, they were either minutes away from freeing their child or having their hopes crushed because they'd been wrong.

Wrong about their child being alive.

Wrong about this location.

Wrong about the source of the Kesins.

I smell several humans.

Kya's angry hiss let Armstrong know she not only smelled humans but also the one who'd tried to steal her Bloodstone and subjected her to a non-consensual C-section.

I also smell Kesins.

"How many?"

From this distance, it's difficult to know for sure. Ten, perhaps more.

Ten mind-controlled dragons were a hell of a lot. He didn't doubt the Bloodstone Dragon could defeat them, but she couldn't just destroy the castle with no thought to the one Kesin they wanted alive and unharmed.

Are you certain your plan will work?

"Not certain. We need to get the Kesins out of the castle, and your presence will make that happen. We also need someone who can slip inside and find our child. I can do that."

He also needed to find the Dracontias stone. That wasn't part of the plan. Kya wouldn't want him endangering his life further. The lack of a healing stone, according to Kya, posed no health risk to their Kesin. The dragon could live fine without it. For Armstrong, that wasn't the point. The stone was a birthright, a genetic gift from the Bloodstone Dragon to her progeny. Armstrong would be damned if he didn't at least try to recover the gemstone for their child.

Kya flew closer to the estate, an ancient warlike structure on sprawling acres of grassland surrounded by high, full trees. Gliding on silent currents, the Bloodstone Dragon circled the castle until she reached the tower house.

The scent of Kesins is strongest here. The dungeon you seek should be beneath the tower house.

Landing then withdrawing her magic binds, Kya lowered her tail so Armstrong could jump off.

He sported a chestnut steel hide double gun shoulder holster with leather harness straps. Two loaded Rugers fit perfectly in each holster. The thumb-break snap and tension screw would allow for a quick draw.

I'm going to bring this castle down. I'll begin at the far end and make as much noise as possible. That should be enough distraction to bring the humans and Kesins out.

Armstrong looked from the castle, ten feet thick walls and forty-foot high, and then back to Kya.

I'm insulted.

"I didn't say anything," he whispered.

That look of yours says much. I'm the Bloodstone Dragon, Armstrong Knight, do not doubt my might.

"Actually, I thought you may bring these stones down on my head before I had a chance to find our child."

I'll destroy the structure and the Kesins slowly. Remember, once you've found our Kesin, send me the image telepathically. When I have a visual of the dungeon, I'll be able to transport the two of you out of there.

Kya had explained how her power to transport worked. She either had to have been to the location before, like when she'd transported Isaiah's children to a home she'd visited many times, or if she had an accurate visual. The second method was less precise and more dangerous. Dragons also didn't transport themselves because that kind of magic worked only on others, which was why Kya hadn't joined his nieces in her fog that fateful day.

Armstrong would prefer to bring their Kesin out himself, but he wasn't sure he'd be able to without Kya's help. Their baby dragon may not trust any human after being held captive by Westmore and Cafferty for eight long years. The dragon may even try to kill him if he got too close.

The formidable door to the tower house was built for defensive purposes. He tried the knob. Locked, of course.

"A little help before you lay siege to the castle, Bloodstone Dragon."

Not that Kya had ever rolled her eyes when she was in human form, but the way she snorted red magic in his face felt equivalent to a DC girl's eye roll.

Armstrong backed up.

With a flick of her gold tail, the door crumbled.

Make haste. I can prolong the battle but so long. Eventually, I'll have to put the Kesins out of their misery.

He should've climbed over the broken door and entered the dark tower house. Instead, he watched the Bloodstone Dragon soar high above the castle, take a deep breath, open her mouth wide and release a stream of raging fire.

He'd never witnessed anything like it outside of a fantasy movie. The Dracontias never displayed this kind of deadly power in public, so moviemakers took liberty with their interpretation. But this, the real thing, was more frightening and majestic than any human manufactured pyrotechnic display.

He saw, for the first time, why the Aragonite Star Dragon had entrusted North America to his youngest Dracontias. The Bloodstone Dragon may have a heart and body of gold, but she also possessed a soul and belly of fire.

Bright red and longer than the dragon, fire shot from her mouth in an intense spray of heat and magic.

Go. Now!

He went, racing into the empty tower house and finding the stairs that led to the underground dungeon. He clicked on his waist-worn flashlight so he wouldn't fall and break his neck on the winding stairs. When he reached the lit wall torches, he turned off the flashlight.

Armstrong heard voices coming from the tower house by the time he reached the last step. He couldn't make out their words, but the sound of footsteps on the stairs had him finding a nook in a wall and hunching down.

"I thought you said she wouldn't be able to track your dragons back here."

"She shouldn't have been able to."

"Well, the goddamn Bloodstone Dragon is here. You saw what she did to the tower house door. It's in pieces."

The voices drew nearer.

"It's fine. She's not down here, which means she still doesn't know where to find her son."

A son? He and Kya had a son. Armstrong's throat tightened at the news, and his heart raced with happiness and fury. These assholes had denied him and Kya their son, and their child the love of his parents. The bastards would pay. But not until they led them to his child.

"Westmore and Cafferty are in the dungeon. Your fire forced the snakes from their hole. Keep up your attack. They should be sending the Kesins your way soon."

"I hope there's enough of your monsters to stop the Bloodstone Dragon. We didn't plan for this."

"I have enough of them, so stop worrying. They'll bring her down, and we'll capture her in dragon form this time. I won't even have to break a saw on her thick skull. Once she sees I control the life of her son, she'll cut the stone out herself and hand it over. As long as we have her hybrid, we control the Bloodstone Dragon."

The voices faded as the men walked away from Armstrong and down the hallway. He could still hear echoes of male voices as he rose from his hiding spot and followed the men.

Armstrong prayed the Kesins's senses weren't as acute as Kya's or that, if they smelled him, they'd lump his scent in with the last two members of the Circle of Drayke.

Keys jangled and then he detected the sound of a heavy door.

He kept to the shadows. Thankfully, the men were familiar with the dungeon, and few torches were lit to guide them.

Pressing himself against a wall, Armstrong held his breath and didn't move when a Kesin bolted past him. Claws scratched stones as the reptile ran past, headed in the direction of the stairs and the exit to the tower house.

The creature roared as it ran farther down the hall and away from its prison.

Armstrong didn't dare move, but he did need air. He let out the breath he'd been holding.

"The first Kesin is on its way."

"Good. I was beginning to bore of knocking down stones younger than my father. I was kind enough to wait until two humans, one male and one female, fled. Servants, I believe. I spared them. They smelled of fear but not of guilt. Ah, I see the Kesin. Yellow-and-red and flying at me."

More Kesins ran past him. He tried to count, but it was damn near impossible to make out one set of footsteps from another. If even one stopped, he would be done for. Luckily, their singular focus sent them down the hall and into the Bloodstone Dragon's snare.

Another time, another place, Kesins may have ruled the ground. But the sky belonged to Afiya dragons.

"I counted fifteen."

"There are twenty, and not all can fly. Wait a few minutes more before pursuing the humans. I do not wish for you to meet one of these beasts in close quarters."

Neither did he.

The sound of roaring, battling dragons shook the tower house above him. Kya said she would give him time, but with twenty dragons attacking her, the longer it took to kill them the more danger she put herself in. Hearing no more claws coming his way, Armstrong crept in the direction where the men had gone.

He rounded a corner and stopped. This corridor was better lit. A row of doors was open. When he reached the first open door, he peered inside. It was as he expected. Empty. He didn't bother inspecting the other cells as he jogged past them. He knew they'd reveal the same.

They'd kept the Kesins in individual cells, which probably meant his son was in a cell, too. The bitter thought had Armstrong pulling the right gun from its holster.

The next corridor, lit as brightly as the last, contained more cells with open doors. Slowing his pace, then stopping when he heard voices again, Armstrong peeked around the corner.

Cafferty leaned against a wall opposite a cell. The door was closed, but it wouldn't be for long. Westmore held a ring with keys in his right hand. He jammed a key into the lock and twisted. The door hissed open and in went the sadistic doctor.

Hugh Cafferty, dressed in nightclothes, a robe and boots, crossed his arms over his chest and pouted like a spoiled brat. "Do you hear that? Her roars are loud and angry enough to topple this castle."

"Be quiet. I need to focus on the stone and the magic within. I've never tried to control this many of them at once, which is why I'm in here with the hybrid. Having him close to the stone makes my job easier."

"Easier?" Cafferty huffed. "He's whining like he's never done before and if he keeps yanking on his shackle, he'll either break his damn neck or pull the chain from the wall. Either result will end with us dead."

No, Kya or his son wouldn't kill them. Armstrong stepped around the corner, raised his gun hand and waited for Cafferty to sense his presence. It didn't take long. The bastard's arms fell to his sides when he spotted him.

Armstrong grinned, showing lots of white teeth. Then shot the bastard in his left shoulder, spinning him around. A bullet to his back. Armstrong closed in on the downed Cafferty. He could've killed him with the first shot. But he wanted the asshole to suffer if only for a few minutes.

A bullet to each leg. No one held his son in shackles as if he were a goddamn slave. Well, if they wanted to treat his son as a slave, then this was a slave uprising.

Armstrong waited for Westmore to come running out of the cell. The man didn't disappoint. He dropped to the ground next to Cafferty, his hands searching for a pulse.

"He's not dead." Westmore, dressed in black slacks and a gray button-down sweater, swung his gaze to Armstrong. "Yet. I'll let him bleed out slowly."

A desperate little roar came from the cell, which had Armstrong clutching his gun and pointing it at the doctor.

"Get your sorry ass up."

Hands covered in Cafferty's blood, Westmore pushed to his feet.

The sound came again. Armstrong wondered if Kya could hear their son's cries. If she could, Cafferty and Westmore would die like Rudolph.

Armstrong walked closer to the men, his body now parallel to the cell. He didn't want to look inside, although he knew he had no other choice if he were to get Kya her visual and help emancipate their son.

"Move." He waved the gun in the direction of the cell.

"Listen, I—"

"Shut the hell up and get your ass in the cell."

Armstrong followed the doctor into the stone prison. The chilly room, about two hundred fifty feet, was bare except for matted hay in a corner. A ring with a thick chain hung from the back wall. At the other end of the chain was a seething red dragon. The end of his tail looked as if it had been dipped in gold.

Metallic gold, like the Bloodstone Dragon.

As wide as a Mastiff but not as thick as one, he weighed about seventy-five pounds and stood twenty-eight inches at the shoulder. The scales at his neck had been rubbed raw from the thick shackle confining him.

He'd wanted answers from Westmore, such as how he'd made the fake Kesins, were there more of them and did anyone else know. Now, he only wanted the cruel doctor dead.

"Where's the stone you stole from my son?"

Westmore dug into his pants pocket and pulled out a red oval-shaped gemstone. He tossed it to Armstrong, who caught the precious jewel and stowed it in his back pocket.

"I found our son."

For long seconds, the sound of battle intensified before silence befell the cold night.

"Do the humans still live?"

"Not for long." For the first time, Armstrong feared the Bloodstone Dragon's wrath. But he had to tell her. *"He's scared, hurt, and chained to a wall. I'm afraid what he'll do if I shoot the chains and free him."*

"He'll attack. Do nothing. I'm on my way."

Kya always spoke with a relaxed, confident cadence, her voice rarely betraying her emotions. It didn't now. But her voice had taken on an extra stillness that didn't bode well for Westmore.

As much as Armstrong itched to put a bullet through the man's non-existent heart, he would do nothing to deny Kya her revenge.

Armstrong snatched the key ring from Westmore's hip. "Where's your office and which key will let me in?"

"The next to the largest key and the last cell at the end of the hall."

He shot Westmore in the kneecap before taking off and smiled when the man screamed. He wouldn't be going anywhere, and the scent of blood would lead Kya straight to the bastard.

Finding the cell, Armstrong let himself inside. This cell was furnished like a doctor's office on one side and a biomedical lab on the other.

Not having time to go through the files and find what he wanted, Armstrong dumped out the contents of a brown moving box and filled it with anything that looked important. Folders. Pictures. Syringes and vials. Medical reports.

Box in hand, he ran back the way he came. Halfway there, the stone ceiling was replaced with crisp night air and the stench of burning bodies. Glancing up, Armstrong watched the entire tower house swirl in a mist of red dragon magic. The structure whipped around like a house caught in a fierce tornado. With each rotation, the tower house crushed in on itself, a rapidly decreasing ball of crumpled stone.

Within mere seconds, little of the huge building remained.

Clutching the box, Armstrong rushed to where he'd left his son and a bleeding Westmore.

Damn, he'd thought Kya would shift and enter the underground tunnel the way he had. How many times did she have to remind him? Kya was the Bloodstone Dragon, and it was the proud, lethal Dracontias who'd laid waste to twenty bloodthirsty Kesins and decimated a centuries-old tower house with jaw-dropping ease.

He knew she would kill Westmore, but the sight of the Bloodstone Dragon hovering over a ceiling-less dungeon, her armored tail through Westmore's open chest, his bloody heart out of his body and impaled on the tip of Kya's gold tail, was enough to have him dropping the box and stumbling inside the cell.

Unlike the first time he'd been in there, his son wild with fright and anger, the red dragon stared in silence at his victorious mother, who gazed upon her baby dragon with awe, relief and love.

Westmore's body and heart slid from Kya's tail, a soft thud on the prison floor.

With a wisp of magic, the shackle around their son's neck snapped and fell. Stained with Westmore's blood, Kya lowered her tail to the baby dragon, encircling his small body. Releasing a heart aching wail, their son collapsed onto Kya's tail.

He's so small and weak. If I could kill the doctor again, I would. Gather whatever you have in that box of yours and meet me where the tower house used to be.

For a minute, he failed to respond. Their dragon had endured much. No child should live as he had. Another year, maybe six months, he would've likely died from malnutrition or a broken neck.

But he hadn't, Armstrong was forced to remind himself when Kya lifted their child's listless form from the cell and to her. She cradled him with a tenderness typical of the Dracontias.

By the time Armstrong climbed the stairs with the brown box and made it to Kya's side, she lay with their son on the grass. Dead Kesins littered the ground, and Cafferty Castle burned in the background.

"He's safe."

Kya nudged him with her snout until she had Armstrong wrapped in her tail beside their sleeping dragon. When she blew on them, Bloodstone magic forming a thick fog, Armstrong knew he wouldn't be riding on Kya's back or taking an international flight home.

Our son is safe because you are a true diata.

CHAPTER FOURTEEN

*"**THIS IS UNPRECEDENTED,** daughter."*

"Yes, thank you for your kindness toward the Knight family."

From the sky, Kya and her father watched the Knights on the beach below. The Southern Coast of Buto was breathtaking from the sky and on the ground. In the Indian Ocean and southeast of Africa, Buto, home to the Dracontias, boasted the best beaches in the world, crystal clear blue waters and white sands. Until six months ago, no human had laid eyes on the Ekon Shore.

"We're all family, Kya. The Knights and the Dracontias."

"You've changed."

The Aragonite Star Dragon's tail came up to circle Kya and pull her close.

"An old dragon I may be but a blind fool I am not. Your diata loves you and your Kesin. Have you told him dragons mate for life?"

"I have not."

She also hadn't told Armstrong he was her mate. That, when she'd lain with him and accepted the human inside her untouched body, he'd became her kendi. The Bloodstone Dragon's forever love.

"He's come to me. As the oldest Dracontias and your father, Armstrong Knight has asked for a wish."

"He had no right."

"He has every right. Armstrong's a father who doesn't want to lose his son again. He's also a man who wishes to forge a family from the charred horrors of the past."

"The sacrifice is too great. The danger even more so."

Shifting, Kya ran the side of her face over her father's. As she continued to grow into a mature dragon, she would inherit more of her father's powers. She would never match the Aragonite Star Dragon's size, but she would duplicate his all-gold form.

For the Dracontias, only one pure gold dragon could exist at a time. That dragon would rule the Dracontias and Buto.

"With Armstrong Knight the human, you can only produce more Kesins. Yet, if he survived the shift, as an Afiya, the gold Dracontias bloodline would not end with you."

One gold hatchling. Out of eight baby dragons between the Aragonite Star Dragon and the Bluestone Dragon, only one had been born with the definable gold scales of Akata, the dragon who would bring strength to the Stones of Dracontias. When the balance of her scales turned gold, her father would cease to exist and Kya, the Bloodstone Dragon, would ascend to Akata, ruler of the Dracontias.

She barely had any green scales left.

Kya buried her face in her father's neck, a childish display not befitting her status or age.

"I'm still Akata, daughter. I am here. Let me gift you with an Afiya who can rule by your side. A kendi worthy of your love and trust."

"Allow me to speak with Armstrong first."

"As you wish, Bloodstone Dragon. Are you ready to name your Kesin and introduce him to the Dracontias?"

After the rescue, she'd transported her baby dragon and Armstrong to his DC home. When she'd arrived and shifted into her human form, Armstrong had already carried their Kesin upstairs and into the nursery he'd decorated years before. A human child's bed replaced the crib she'd last seen in the room, but most everything else remained the same.

Kya hadn't been able to speak when she saw Armstrong curled around their sleeping child, unafraid he would awaken, startled and attack. He'd whispered apologies into their Kesin's ear and stroked his soft baby dragon skin the way Kya's father did to his hatchlings.

The next morning, Armstrong had awoken to a human child in his arms. Their son was short and thin with a heart-tightening resemblance to his father.

Her diata had wept.

So had Kya, who'd watched over them the entire night.

An hour later, he'd shifted back into his dragon form. A week after that, she'd returned home with her Kesin and Armstrong Knight. He'd pled his case, asking to stay on Buto for a few months to get to know his son. She couldn't deny him his request, no matter how painful she knew the eventual parting would be for them all.

Half a year later, their Kesin healthy and happy, the time for the naming and Armstrong's return to the land of the humans was upon them.

Kya flew away from her father and toward the beach below. As she did so, the bright sky darkened with the appearance of every Dracontias on Buto. The few Kesins born to an Afiya and human, over the centuries, were also in the morning sky. Dracontias magic held them aloft. Their lack of a healing stone made them no less a Dracontias and beloved dragon of Buto.

The Knights reclined on the chairs and under a wooden cabana with flowing white curtains on the top and sides that rustled in the wind and shielded them from the rays of the sun. Kya's siblings had assigned themselves the task of making the Knights stay on Buto as comfortable as possible for the humans. They'd begun with Armstrong, who wanted for nothing during the six months of his stay. He didn't seem to miss the creature comforts that came with living in a home with electricity, and he appreciated the cabin Gasira and Ledisi gifted to him.

Kya had no idea where her siblings retrieved the wooden structure from, but it had a fireplace, which warmed Armstrong on cool Buto nights. The spacious, one-level cabin's open floor plan reduced their Kesin's anxiety of closed-in places when he stayed with his father instead of sleeping under the stars and curled in the circle of Kya's body. Most nights, however, Armstrong would toss his double sleeping bag beside Kya, slip inside and then wait for their baby dragon to make himself comfortable on the rest of the bag.

On some of those nights, Kya and Armstrong would awaken to ten wiggling toes and two playful hands. The transformation never lasted long, an hour or two at most. Unsurprisingly, Armstrong treated and loved their Kesin the same no matter his form.

Kya landed next to Armstrong, quite handsome in a black suit and tie and white dress shirt he'd insisted on wearing for the occasion. Dark, bare feet peeked out from under black dress pants, and he laughed every time their son tickled his toes with his wet tongue.

Glancing from father to son, Kya worried their Kesin would retreat into his shell after Armstrong departed for the land of humans. They'd bonded in a way Kya hoped but didn't think possible between a Kesin and their human parent. Perhaps Armstrong could reach their son because he'd spent so much time around the Bloodstone Dragon. More likely, Kya reasoned, sitting on her haunches and using her tail to pull her son to rest under her front legs, the Dracontias's fear of their secret being revealed prevented many a human parent from having the opportunity to develop a relationship with their Kesin.

She peered up at the Dracontias, Afiyas and Kesins. Her kind thought themselves intelligent and enlightened beings, and they were, but they'd also allowed fear of exposure to cloud their judgment and deny Kesins the love of their human parent. In her ignorance and cowardice, she would've done the same. Still, her experience with the Circle of Drayke couldn't be ignored or dismissed. Some humans did pose a threat to the Dracontias and more would if the dragons revealed too much or made themselves vulnerable.

Humans outnumbered the Dracontias, but a war between them would leave the Earth in ruins and the humans an endangered species. The Aragonite Star Dragon's rules were meant to prevent such possibilities, and Kya couldn't deny his mandates had fostered peaceful relations between the two species.

Yet, the heart was unpredictable and not subject to a ruler's protective dictates. When the time came for Kya to serve as Akata, she hoped she'd rule wisely and fairly, as the Aragonite Star Dragon had done for over two thousand years.

Is there anything you wish to say to those gathered before I begin?

"Am I supposed to say something? Give a speech? If so, you should've told me because I have nothing prepared."

Since when does a Knight require advanced notice to speak?

"Aren't you the funny dragon? For your information, I'm here as a silent observer."

Oh, you're being quite good today, Armstrong Knight. That suit and your feigned compliance become you. But it will not last. I'll give you an hour.

"An hour for what?"

A hand rose to stroke her side, a back and forth movement that, if performed by one of her siblings, would've sent familial warmth through Kya. With Armstrong, however, his touches created a decidedly intimate heat within her. He'd learned too much from Gasira about the female dragon form, including how and where to caress Kya to produce his desired effect.

Thirty seconds. You were good for thirty seconds. Do remove your hand from my side.

"No one knows what I'm doing. Besides, you make the most amazing sound when I scratch you here."

Before action met words, Kya toughened her scales. Not enough to harm Armstrong's hand but enough so she wouldn't embarrass herself in front of those gathered.

He laughed. "You're adorable. I'll be good."

For how long?

"How long is the naming ceremony?"

A snort preceded her answer. *No more than five minutes. We dragons don't require pomp and circumstance.*

"Well, there you go. Five minutes." Two hands slapped together. "Better get on with it, Bloodstone Dragon, the Dracontias and Knights await."

Kya would miss him when he returned to his human life, which he'd put on hold to be with her and their son on Buto.

She projected her words into everyone's mind, including the Knights.

On this day of Amadi, we rejoice because our family is made stronger by the addition of a Kesin, a bridge between humans and dragons. A bridge between the Knights and the Akata family. Armstrong, come forth and introduce your son.

No longer playful, a serious Armstrong walked around Kya and stood in front but to the left of their son. His hand settled at the nape of the baby dragon's neck, where it caressed in smooth, soothing circles.

Their son snuggled against Armstrong's side, content to stay pressed between his parents.

"I once knew a human who became sick. The doctors tried their best, but there was little they could do to save him. He had four children and a wife who loved him dearly."

From her seat in the cabana, Mrs. Knight began to weep. Isaiah, to her left, laced his fingers through his mother's.

"For months, I watched him wither. His body weakened but never his courageous spirit and indomitable light. When he passed away, he took them with him. Six months ago, I felt both when I entered a cell not fit for any living creature." His face lowered and kissed the head of their son. "My mother believes in signs from God. That night and in that cell, I sensed my father's presence. I believe he kept my son safe when I couldn't. Cancer may have claimed his life, but it didn't break his spirit or heart. Awful men may have caged this little Kesin's body, but they didn't break his spirit or heart. He endured. Survived. I name my son Elijah Isaiah Knight."

Knees dropped to the sand and arms embraced. "Welcome to the Knight family, Elijah. Your grandfather would be proud. I know you'll wear his name well."

Armstrong stood and received hugs and kisses from his family, but none more than from his weeping mother.

Kya moved backward so the Knights could shower Elijah with the same affection. He glanced over his shoulder at her to make sure she hadn't gone too far but otherwise stayed where he was and accepted the coddling.

"You said you were unprepared to make a speech."

"It wasn't a speech. I spoke from my heart."

"Yes, I'm aware. You've made your family happy, Armstrong, especially your mother."

Armstrong turned to wink at Kya. *"I could give you more Kesins. That would make Mom really happy."* He winked again then laughed when Kya failed to respond.

He teased and tempted but could Armstrong not see all he'd give up if he entered into a permanent relationship with Kya and the Dracontias. The Knights were the exception not the new rule on Buto. As much as she loved her diata, Kya couldn't take him from his human family.

Despite all that had changed since Kya first realized she was pregnant, much had not. Their Kesin wasn't equipped to live among humans. If he ever learned to control his shift, it would take him at least a century to do so. In less time than that, the remainder of her green scales would be gone as would be her father and Armstrong.

Eventually, the Knights returned to the cabana, with Armstrong filling the vacant seat to his mother's right. Flanked by her sons and surrounded by her daughters and grandchildren, Mrs. Knight beamed.

Kya would continue to watch over the older human woman. Armstrong's father may have died in pain, with no dragon to cure and extend his life, but Kya wouldn't allow Mrs. Knight to suffer the same fate. When her time came, she would drift from life and into death, her human heaven her eternal reward.

Are you ready, Elijah?

Her brave son rarely spoke telepathically, but he understood everything said to him. Elijah scrambled to her. His gold tipped tail slapped against the sand, his red face upturned.

My anxious son. After today, you'll have everything denied to you on the day of your birth, thanks to your father.

Once again, Kya projected her thoughts to the crowd. Unlike Armstrong, Kya had little to say.

A healing stone does not make a dragon a Dracontias. Yet, a Stone of Dracontias offers each dragon an opportunity to help those in need.

The morning of their return from Ireland, Armstrong had presented Kya with Elijah's Dracontias stone along with a box of information on their baby dragon he didn't want to risk falling into the wrong hands. After Armstrong had read every file, she'd burned the contents of the box and kept the stone.

Kya lowered her nose to her son's forehead. He stayed still as her Bloodstone magic seeped from her and into him. On its wispy tentacles, she withdrew his stone from her skull and, with care, used her magic to travel up his nasal passage and to the protective cavity of his brain. The tentacles located the hollow in his skull where his Stone of Dracontias had once been.

A gentle push of magic had the tentacles inserting the healing stone into the hollow.

Elijah stumbled forward when the first whoosh of Dracontias magic whipped through his tiny body. His magic. Red like Kya's but not from a Bloodstone.

You'll grow used to the magic and your healing stone. I'll teach you, the way my parents taught me.

Kya coiled her tail around her baby dragon and lifted into the air. The Dracontias, much like the Knights, awaited her choice of a dragon name. Well, as Armstrong once told her, Bloodstone Dragon wasn't a name but a title and Elijah would receive his much earlier than was normal.

She raised her son high into the air so all the Dracontias could see. He vibrated crimson, his returned stone adding luster to already bright scales.

Kesin. Human. Dracontias.

Let us rejoice and welcome the Red Jasper Dragon and his healing stone of courage and wisdom.

Below, the Knights cheered. In the sky, a rainbow of magic burst from the Dracontias, radiant streams of love. The colorful mists scooped Elijah from Kya's tail and tossed him into the air. On winds of magic, Elijah was handed from one Dracontias to the next, beginning with the Aragonite Star Dragon and the Bluestone Dragon.

Each dragon ran the tip of their tail or tongue over the baby dragon. For eight years, her son had known nothing but cruelty and loneliness. He'd been touch deprived, which hurt Kya's heart.

Seeing him now, basking in the affection of his family, safe and happy and where he belonged, the human inside of the Bloodstone Dragon sobbed tears of joy.

CHAPTER FIFTEEN

ARMSTRONG PACED HIS living room. He'd heard everything Kya had said, none of which surprised him. He'd even agreed with her, which did nothing for his bad mood and the sense of desperation rampaging up and down his spine.

Elijah slept in the twin bed he'd hastily purchased for him before he and Kya had set off for southern Ireland. For years, everyone told Armstrong he should stop torturing himself and pack up the nursery. They'd all thought his son dead. Most days, so had he. Yet whenever he attempted to close the door on that chapter of his life, stubborn hope would reassert itself. Thus, the nursery never again became his home office, and his son would always have a place in his home, even if a rarely used bedroom.

He hadn't been in his house for half a year, and it felt stale and claustrophobic. Armstrong wasn't the outdoors type, but he'd been shocked by how easily he'd adapted to life on Buto with the dragons. Admittedly, he missed television, music and fast food. He did learn how to grill meats and vegetables like a champ and his body, from running after a baby dragon with an endless supply of energy, had an impressive muscular cut he hadn't seen since he turned thirty-seven and his metabolism began to slow.

Dressed in worn jeans and an old T-shirt, Armstrong plopped on the couch a cushion length down from Kya, who looked as awful as he felt. Well, at least that was something he supposed.

He shifted to his side to face Kya, who leaned against the armrest of the couch, her legs pulled to her chest. Physically, she'd changed little in the twenty-two years they'd known each other. Even if she'd never become pregnant with Elijah, this would've been their fate. He would've continued to grow old while she stayed young and beautiful.

Armstrong had his forty-seventh birthday while on Buto. He'd known men who'd dated women twenty years their junior. Some guys were even stupid enough to leave their wife for a younger woman. While he, like any man, enjoyed the sight of a beautiful woman, youth and vitality couldn't replace the depth of pleasure that came with knowing someone for years and loving that person, all the more, for the time shared together.

Still, he possessed enough vanity to not want Kya to see him grow old while she went from looking like his lover to his daughter and finally to his grand-daughter. Kya was a dragon, but she was also human enough to appreciate the virility of a male's body.

"Your father agreed to turn me into a dragon. According to Westmore's files, if a human consumes the blood of a dragon, the shift will take place. That's how he was able to create the Kesins."

"Father has never turned any human into a dragon. Westmore was insane, and so were his monsters. Do you wish to become like them, Armstrong, a mindless beast of prey?"

"Westmore theorized the blood and stone of a full-dragon would mediate the negative effects he experienced with the Kesins. That's why he and Cafferty turned their attention back to capturing you. They wanted a pureblood source, no offense to Elijah."

"Did you not hear me when I said Kenneth Westmore was insane? You cannot entrust your life to the hypothesis of a madman."

"What if he's right?"

Even in human form, when upset, Kya released wisps of Bloodstone magic from her nose.

"What if he's wrong? Do you know what that will mean?" Her voice rose, and the hands on her knees fisted. "It means if you shift into a bloodthirsty Afiya, which is so much worse than an out-of-control Kesin, I'll be forced to kill you."

"I know."

In a blur of dragon speed, Kya was in his face and straddling his hips. "You know nothing, Armstrong Knight. You always think you do, but you do not. Harming you would destroy the Bloodstone Dragon and the human that is Kya. I would rather watch you grow old and die than kill my son's father and my mate."

"Your kendi."

"Gasira talks too much. But yes, you're my kendi."

"Forever love. That's what I want us to have, Kya. And there's only one way for us to have what we both want."

She shook her head and tears formed but didn't fall. "It's too dangerous. I won't permit it."

"It's my choice."

"A selfish choice."

"How is wanting to spend centuries with you and Elijah a selfish choice?"

Armstrong slid his hands into Kya's long, thick hair. They hadn't been this physically close in years, she in human form and them alone in their house the way they once were.

"It's selfish because there's no guarantee of success. If the transformation doesn't go as you hope, your death will bring pain to your family. Is that what you want, for your mother to bury her son as she did her husband?"

Pulling her even closer, Armstrong laid his forehead against hers. "You know it isn't. I don't want to leave my family. No more than I want to lose you and Elijah. Help me find a way to have both. So yeah, call me a selfish human, but I want to have both."

He kissed her, the way he'd wanted to do for months. But Kya, like all the Dracontias, he'd learned, rarely shifted into their human form while on Buto. They were, as she'd said many times, dragons who could simply transform into a human.

But there, in their home and on his lap, Armstrong took what his mate willingly gave.

Kya kissed him back with the same hunger lust surging through him. She tasted so good, her tongue in his mouth, exploring and driving him wild. His gray-and-white shirt ripped under her impatient hands. And the buttons of her blouse popped under his.

Before he knew it, they were upstairs, on the bed, lights off and the bedroom door closed. They finished undressing each other as best they could while refusing to stop kissing.

He worked his way down Kya's amazing body, sucking her neck, fondling breasts, and flicking nipples.

Throaty moans and writhing hips had Armstrong planting open-mouthed kisses on her taut stomach, curvy hips, and soft inner thighs. Kissing his way back up to her waiting lips, Armstrong's fingers played with her springy nest of curls, his thumb rubbing the supple folds of her sex.

Kya moaned into his mouth and swallowed his tongue deep, just as his fingers slipped inside her. Probing, thrusting, and crooking to find the ridges to her pleasure he remembered all too well.

Wrenching her mouth from his and breathing hard, Kya arched her back, drove her sex onto his thick fingers and came in a burst of dragon magic and human cries of release.

Hands going to his face and cradling, Kya opened green jasper eyes and smiled. "I'd forced myself to not think how good you could make my human body feel." A lick of his lips and then a bite to his chin. "I tingle all over. It's a delicious sensation." With dragon strength, she shifted them. Armstrong on his back and Kya above him on her knees, their groins pressed intimately close. "I remember what you like and how to please you."

"Got to love that photographic memory of yours."

Kya took him inside, she wet and pulsing, he hard and throbbing. Hands rose and gripped her waist, hips lifted and pressed.

No condom

He stopped. Swore.

Kya leaned down and kissed him, her nipples grazing his chest. "What's wrong?" Not waiting for an answer, she began to move over top of him. Short thrusts to the tip of his penis, then back up. Short thrusts, then back up. One deep slide, a grind and then back up.

The short thrusts decreased as the long slides onto him increased. By the time she reached ten deep slides, Armstrong was close to coming and had almost forgotten about his lack of a condom.

"Kya, wait."

She began again with nine short thrusts and one deep slide. Eight short thrusts and two deep slides. Damn, she was going to kill him and get herself with another Kesin.

He wanted that. He really did. To tie his Bloodstone Dragon to him with another child. She would have to give in then, right? Wrong. He wouldn't do that to her or to himself.

"Kya, I'm not wearing a condom."

"I know." She sat up, grabbed his wrists, lifted his hands to her breasts and continued to ride him. Eyes closed and head fell back on soft, persistent groans. "A Dracontias can conceive only once every two hundred or so years, regardless of our form."

Disappointment welled in him, but he knew it was for the best. Unless Armstrong were turned into a dragon, he and Kya wouldn't have another child.

"How many years before you're next able to conceive?"

Glassy, passion-filled eyes opened and stared down at him. Not answering, Kya stretched her body over his. Greedy hands went to her ass and helped her rock against him.

"By the human calendar, I've lived for two hundred fifty years, which is quite young for a dragon."

"You're sexy for an old lady."

She laughed, then moaned when he spread his legs and thrust upward.

"And tight."

He did it again.

"And wet."

Armstrong was so close. From her harsh breaths, so was Kya.

"A compromise, Bloodstone Dragon."

"Mmmm, not now. Later."

Knowing she wouldn't listen to him as long as she was on top and in the power position, Armstrong flipped them over. Not as smoothly as Kya had done but he'd stayed inside her, which was all that mattered.

Her growl of annoyance had him wrapping Kya's right leg around his hip and driving into her with long, deep thrusts. In a matter of seconds, her growls evened out to pleased groans.

"A compromise." Armstrong stopped and waited for Kya's eyes to focus on him. When they did, he said again, "A compromise. Please."

Her hands cradled his face again. "What's the compromise?"

"I won't accept my wish from the Aragonite Star Dragon. I'll live what's left of my human life, spending as much time with you and Elijah as your duties to Buto will allow. In exchange, Kya, I only ask, when I'm old with a well-lived life behind me, you'll come to me and grant my wish. I know the compromise doesn't solve the issue of the possibility of Westmore being wrong. I don't know how to get around that except to say, if the worst happens and you have to kill me, you'll know you haven't denied me life but given me the death I earned."

The tears she hadn't let fall when they were downstairs dropped now. Down the sides of her face, over her ears and onto the pillow below her head.

"The first night on the rooftop of my apartment building, you asked me to be your human guide, a cross-cultural exchange you couldn't fully offer in return. As a compromise, you agreed to grant me one wish and two questions. Since then, you've given me so many wishes, some I didn't deserve or shouldn't have expected from you. And you've answered hundreds of my questions except for the one I've never been brave enough to ask because dragons don't marry."

More tears fell, and Armstrong began to push into Kya again, unable to deny them this rare stolen moment of carnal delight.

"You have always asked for too much."

"I never asked for anything before I met you. As a child, I forced myself to accept the absence of my father in my life. With you, Kya, I can't breathe for wanting you so much. Your bloodstone does more than heals. It brings love and grounds negative energy. I have faith in the power of your Stone of Dracontias, not because of what Westmore hypothesized but because I know my wish is also yours."

Armstrong made love to Kya, channeling his hopes and dreams for a shared Dracontias future into giving her pleasure and multiple orgasms.

He grunted as he came, sweaty and loud and blissed out of his mind.

A floorboard outside of the closed door creaked. "Dad-dy?"

Wait. Had his son just—Armstrong, naked and partially erect, bolted out of bed and rushed to the door. He would've opened it too, as he was if a composed Kya hadn't used her magic to dress him in boxers and a T-shirt.

He opened the door and smiled down at his son. He'd gone to bed as a dragon and now stood, sleepy-eyed and the size of a five-year-old.

Armstrong didn't think he would ever get used to the difference between human and dragon development. Thin but strong arms raised. Armstrong didn't hesitate to pick up his son and bring him into the bedroom.

"He spoke."

"Yes, I heard."

"He said daddy. All my hard work paid off. Elijah's first word was daddy."

"As I said, I heard."

"You're jealous."

As usual, when he said something ridiculous, Kya ignored him. In a blink, she'd done away with the sex-scented sheets and replaced them with fresh linen. They both smelled of sex, which, thankfully, Elijah wouldn't know.

Armstrong settled himself and his son under the covers. Elijah went straight to his mother the moment his knees hit the mattress. She wore a sexy red nightgown he planned to strip off her come morning. That was if he could get their son back into his bed without waking him.

Tucked against Kya and between them, Elijah wasted no time falling asleep, one hand fisted in his mother's hair, the other in his mouth, sucking his thumb.

He'd worry about the boy having buck teeth if he kept that up, but Elijah was a healing dragon. His teeth would be just fine.

Armstrong caught Kya's gaze over their son's head, a mass of hair the child hated to have combed, but Kya refused to have cut.

"A compromise?"

"Yes," he answered.

On a long put-upon sigh, Kya, the Bloodstone Dragon, future leader of Buto and mother to his child, rolled her eyes like a true Knight female. "Fine. We have a compromise. If I'm forced to kill you, Armstrong Knight, I'll make it bloody and quite painful."

"I love you, too. I'll never ask for another wish."

"Liar."

"Okay, maybe one tiny wish in a hundred fifty years when you're ovulating again or whatever happens to female dragons when they're ready to conceive."

———◦———

Present-Day

"Mother, it's time."

"I know."

Kya's eyes drifted from Armstrong's weathered face and to Elijah who held his father in his arms. She'd heard humans say, about the ninety-two-year-old Armstrong Knight, that he "looked good for his age." To Kya, her kendi appeared frail and exhausted. Death danced around the corners of dull brown eyes that sagged more than focused.

She thought she prepared herself well for this moment. The way tears slipped from her and hands shook, Kya knew she had not. Her diata could die tonight. If she did nothing, his human form would succumb to age. If she transformed him and he turned in a mindless Afiya, he would be lost to her and Elijah forever.

"It's what Dad wants."

"I know." Eyes that reminded her so much of Armstrong stared back at Kya, watery and afraid. "You do not need to be here. Everyone will watch over your father."

Elijah shifted his father in his arms and glanced around the clearing. The entire Akata family stood in front of Armstrong's cabin home on Buto. In honor of the human they all loved, they'd gathered in their human form to say farewell to the man they knew and, if all went well, to welcome a new Dracontias to their family.

"I know I'm young, but I'd like to stay. Please, Mother."

Kya should make Elijah return to the Eshe Forest until it was done. She didn't want his last memory of his father to be that of a ravaging dragon his mother had to put down like a rabid dog.

Like his father, Kya could deny Elijah little.

"Place your father onto the sleeping bag, then step back."

With careful movements, Elijah bent to one then two knees and set-tled Armstrong onto the black sleeping bag he'd had for years. For several minutes, the young dragon held his father's hand and didn't move. He understood, like all gathered, his father might not survive what was to come.

Kya gave her son the time he needed to say what could be his final words to Armstrong.

"I love you, Dad."

Weak, Armstrong raised a hand to Elijah's cheek and wiped away his tears. "I know. You're the best son a man could've ever hoped to have. If I cannot, take care of your mother for me. She'll grumble that she's the Bloodstone Dragon and can take care of herself. It's a partial truth. Stay by her side and listen to her words of wisdom. She's the smartest person I know."

Elijah laughed, pressed his cheek into his father's palm, and then with slumped shoulders stood.

"Come closer, Kya. I can barely see you."

No, not prepared at all for this moment. Armstrong understood the risks and had tried, since Kya brought him to Buto a week ago, to get her to speak with him about it so they could say their farewells. She'd refused. But she could no longer.

Kya dropped to her knees beside Armstrong. "Don't make me say goodbye."

"Not goodbye, my Bloodstone Dragon. Never goodbye. Three words. You've only said them once. I'd like to hear them again."

Leaning over Armstrong, loose hair a curtain of black around his face, Kya kissed his forehead. His cheeks. His lips. "I love you."

"And I love you. I've lived a good life, Kya, much of it because of you and our son. I have no regrets, if this is the end. Any life I may get to live after this one is a bonus. So, don't cry, my love. I'll always be your diata."

Heart in her throat, Kya stood and stepped away from Armstrong. She didn't trust Westmore. The man's thought processes hadn't worked like most humans. Yet, he had achieved something no Dracontias knew was possible.

Kya had learned much from the Aragonite Star Dragon, who stood next to Elijah. Dragons, though powerful as one, were invincible as a group with a single-minded purpose. Today, Armstrong's safe transition from human to Afiya was the Akata family's single-minded purpose.

If Westmore thought the magic from one Afiya's Stone of Dracontias would produce a mentally stable dragon, then Kya reasoned the combined magic and might of ten would be that much stronger.

Elijah's blood may have resulted in a weak, impure version of a Kesin, but Kya had no intention of plying Armstrong with dragon's blood. She may not have prepared for his passing, but Kya had given his transformation much thought.

If she didn't succeed, it wouldn't be because Kya failed to dissect and address every option before deciding on the best plan of action.

Her family, all except Elijah, who ran onto the cabin's front porch for his safety, transformed into dragons. Kya did as well. As one, they lifted fifty feet into the air, a circle of gold and green dragons around the form of Armstrong Knight.

In unison, they blew wisps of healing stone magic from their nostrils and onto her diata.

Bloodstone.

Aragonite.

Lapis Lazuli.

Sunstone.

Soul Stone.

Jade.

Amethyst.

Carnelian.

Onyx.

Citrine.

Ten Stones of Dracontias, one mighty fog of transformative healing magic.

Human science could never duplicate this, the giving of stone magic to birth an Afiya with a Stone of Dracontias.

Kya saw the stone take form in the center of the magical fog. Armstrong's stone, golden-brown with a silky luster.

Collectively, they pushed the fog and gemstone downward. The stone would have to accept Armstrong and he the stone.

Kya heard Armstrong's deep intake of breath. He coughed. Choked. The fog formed a funnel, the tip of which was in Armstrong's mouth. With labored gulps, he sucked down the stone and the magical fog.

It was done then.

Lowering to the ground, Kya and her family, still in a protective circle around Armstrong's prone human body, they waited.

"What's going on? I can't see anything. Is Dad all right?"

"I don't yet know. Be patient. If you must, transform and come sit behind me. You may not enter or join the circle, however."

Her son transformed quicker than she'd known him to do. Soon enough, Kya felt his smaller frame snuggled against her lower back.

"Comfortable, Red Jasper Dragon?"

"Yes, what will be Dad's Dracontias name?"

"Tiger's Eye Dragon. Willpower, confidence, and good fortune."

"It suits him."

Kya agreed. But Armstrong hadn't yet shifted, and he no longer breathed.

Two excruciating hours later, the transformation began. Wrinkled skin, gray hair, and brittle bones curled in on themselves as golden-brown magic seeped from Armstrong's eyes, nose, and ears and engulfed the human.

Elijah stirred where he'd fallen asleep against Kya and tried to peer between Kya and Ledisi and to see what Kya could only gaze upon with awe and rapture.

From the golden-brown fog of magic emerged a dark-brown Afiya, his chest and legs golden-brown and his eyes, which repeatedly blinked at the dragon's around him, were a rich shade of gold.

At that moment, Kya was sure she didn't breathe. The thirty-foot dragon of muscle and might stood tall and strong, and Kya was afraid to trust the sanity she saw in the eyes that found hers.

Unable not to, she inched forward, which gave Elijah enough room to dart past her and straight to the large golden-brown dragon.

The red dragon skidded to a halt. Instinctively, Kya began to reach for her son with her tail.

"Let me. I've always wanted to hold our son the way you do."

Excited, Elijah squealed when Armstrong wrapped his golden-brown tail around him and lifted until father and son were face-to-face.

Her family drifted away, leaving Kya alone with her son and dragon mate.

"You did it. I never doubted you, Kya. Not for one minute. Thank you."

He may not have. But she'd certainly doubted herself.

"So, this is what it's like to be a dragon. Except for looking down on everything, I feel the same."

Only Armstrong Knight could manage the impossible and make such an outrageous claim.

Kya closed the distance between herself and Armstrong, Elijah pressed between them. Her head fell to Armstrong, and she caressed him in the way of familial dragons. Later, she would show Armstrong how mated dragons touched.

"Will you teach me all there is to know about being a dragon?"

"Of course. For a fee."

"A fee?" Armstrong placed Elijah on the ground, and the dragon ran around their legs, hyper and happy. *"What kind of fee?"*

"Hmm, I don't yet know."

Armstrong returned her caress, his tail finding the spot on her side he knew sent flutters of pleasure through her.

"When you figure it out, let me know. In the meantime, teach me how to fly."

Elijah jumped onto Armstrong's back and scrambled up his body until his neck lay propped on the top of his father's head.

"Flying takes a lot of concentration, Dad." Elijah cut his red eyes at Kya, lowered his voice and whispered into his father's ear as if she couldn't hear him. *"Mother is a stern instructor. Believe it or not, she's worse than grandfather."*

"Oh, really? Well, I can't wait for your mother's lessons."

He winked, a gesture she'd never seen by a dragon.

"Say it again, Kya."

"I just said it."

"That's when I was human Armstrong Knight. I want to hear it as the Tiger's Eye Dragon."

"It will sound the same."

"I don't think it will. Say it again."

Kya increased her pace, leaving Armstrong behind her. *"You want too much,"* she threw over her shoulder.

"I've only ever wanted you. I love you, Bloodstone Dragon."

Kya stopped, waited for Armstrong to catch up. They faced each other, and she blew Bloodstone magic in his face.

"And I've only ever wanted you. Now and forever."

THE END

EXCLUSIVE SNEAK PEAK-DRAGON LORE AND LOVE: ISIS AND OSIRIS

Prologue

The Dragon Kingdom of Nebty

FORESTS BURNED, DRAGONS roared, and wings flapped in a deadly cacophony of violence and war.

Dragons of all sizes and colors were in the air and on the ground, battling to the death over who would control the twin deity scepters of Wadget and Nekhbet.

Nut, a blue-and-white sky dragon with a long snout, curled tail, and two horns on her head that curved back at the tip, stared up at her mate with frosty eyes of rebuttal.

Geb, a powerful green-and brown two-headed earth dragon with red eyes, spikey armored scales, and a whipping tail that ended with a flat arrowhead perfect for cutting and impaling, glared down at her. At the height of one hundred twenty-eight feet, Nut, half her mate's size, growled at him when he used his massive head to shove her to the mouth of the Cave of Dep.

"You stay here and protect the hatchlings," he ordered, as if the twin goddesses had left the earth dragon as the sole ruler of Nebty and guardian of the Gateway of the Two Ladies. They hadn't. Nut and Geb ruled together. Some days, like today, when the inevitable war for power and dominance erupted, Geb's protective nature made him high-handed and unyielding.

Glancing behind her at the cracked white shell and to the baby dragons huddled behind the fragments, Nut understood Geb's position, although the thought of leaving her mate set the fire in her belly to boiling.

"If I fall in battle, your sky magic and ferocity will be all that stands between the foolish among us from getting their claws on the scepters."

"I know." Nut stepped closer to her mate, her snout going to one of his thick necks and rubbing. *"It's not just our dragon betrayers who*

want the power of the scepters that you must defeat, but the Demon Kingdom who seeks unfettered access to the human realm."

That was as close as Nut would come to acknowledging the very real possibility her mate may not survive this dark and dangerous night. For years, the Demon Kingdom, led by King Sansabonsom, had sought to undermine the rules set forth by the goddesses after they'd sought eternal rest within the scepters, leaving Nut and Geb as the gatekeepers between the preternatural and human realms.

Even as they spoke of Nut fleeing with their daughters and Geb remaining behind, sounds of warfare permeated the cold winter air, echoed by bodies crashing from the sky in flaming scales of defeat.

"Not all want the scepters. The strongest of our allies will stay and fight." Geb lowered his heads and licked Nut's face, an affectionate gesture she feared would be their last. *"I need you to lead the others to safety, especially the young ones. If they stay, I can't guarantee their safety."*

A stream of fire emerged from the darkness and behind Geb. The spray of molten heat slammed into the earth dragon. His wings, instinctively, snapped out and up to shield Nut and their hatchlings. With a bellow of fury, Geb leaped into the air, his wings taking him on a collision course with a lava dragon who possessed none of the earth dragon's size or might.

In a matter of seconds, Geb had one of his mouths locked around the dragon's reddish-black neck, and the other jaw clamped onto a black wing. With a hard tug, the wing and head disconnected from the dragon's body. Magma spurted and oozed. The dead lava dragon smashed to the charred ground with a resounding thud.

Spitting out the wing and head, Geb turned to Nut, who still stood at the mouth of the cave. As they stared at each other, dragons not involved in the war began to move toward her. Most of them were dragon mothers with their hatchlings or dragons too young, old, or small to fight on either side but old enough to help tend to the youngest in their party.

"Take care of them, Nut. Fighting is easy, living and building from the ash of ruin are hard. Be well, my queen. And be safe. Tell my daughters I love the—"

Six dragons attacked Geb. Claws, tails, and fire sent him flying backward but not down and definitely not out of the battle. With an ear-piercing roar of rage, the two-headed earth dragon counterattacked. Fire, wings, and scales collided in the morbid, dark sky, the dragon battle epic in its savagery and sacrilege.

Dragons weren't created to fight each other or intended to use the goddesses' magic for personal gain and short-sighted goals of power and privilege. Yet, anarchy reigned. Her beloved Geb would fight the dragon traitors who would steal the scepters, rule the preternatural realm, and turn a blind eye while the Demon Kingdom invaded the human realm and feasted on the flesh of children.

With a heavy heart, Nut looked away from her heroic mate and to the dragons awaiting her directive. She would lead them to safety, as Geb had ordered. He and his most trusted allies were fighting to give Nut time to get as many dragons through the gateway and into the realm of humans.

With a low rumble, she called her daughters to her. On young, unsteady legs, they came, and she used her tail to lift them onto her back. She took to the sky, leading a caravan of dragons away from the only home they've known and toward the Gateway of the Two Ladies.

Makara, mate to Asir, one of the border guards who'd aligned with the demon king, flew by her side. Her oldest hatchling, Osiris, trailed behind his rock dragon mother, as best he could. Set, Makara's youngest dragon, held onto his mother's back, dark eyes wide and frightened.

Nut heard the demons before she saw them. Not only did demons have a taste for human children, but they were also known to eat the young of any species, including demon hatchlings. The sound of bat wings chased the caravan as they sped through the sky and toward the gateway that would take them to the other side. A few more miles and they would reach their destination.

In no time, two columns with an archway and hieroglyphic writing decorating the divine structure loomed before Nut and her charges. The demons right behind them, three hundred or more, from the sound of their wings.

Nut couldn't risk opening the gateway and having the hordes of demons follow them through.

"What are we going to do?" Makara asked. *"The young ones are exhausted. If the demons catch up to us, they won't have enough energy to fight or flee."*

Nut knew. She'd set a demanding pace from the Cave of Dep and to the Gateway of the Two Ladies. Increasing her speed when the demons began their pursuit. During the race to safety, she'd lost no dragon. Mature dragons had to secure the hatchlings who'd started out flying under their own power and load them onto their backs. Makara had wasted no time coiling her strong, long tail around Osiris's winded body and setting him behind his younger brother, who cowered between his mother's rock indentations and wept like the terrified three-year-old he was.

Not questioning the ramifications of her plan, Nut called to the two border guards stationed at the gateway, both ice dragons. They responded with a quickness that gave Nut renewed hope.

"Yes, my queen."

"An ice wall between them and us. Now."

"Yes, my queen."

"Will the ice stop them?" Makara watched the ice dragons fly past the group, her question likely shared by others.

"Not for long and not without my help. Do you have room for two more passengers?"

Before Makara could reply, Aset, a fifteen-year-old shadow dragon, young yet big for her age, answered. *"I'll take the princesses, my queen."*

Under different circumstances, Nut wouldn't entertain the thought of having such a young and inexperienced dragon serve in the role of protector for her hatchlings. But these times demanded decisive action, earned trust, and unflinching faith.

Aset's parents, members of Geb's personal guard, were back there, fighting for not only Nebty and the human realm, but for all preternaturals who would be threatened if the demons controlled their realm.

Nut turned her daughters over to Aset, who used her shadow magic to blend into the darkness. Even she could barely see the onyx dragon.

Unburdened, Nut turned to face the three demon hordes. The ice dragons, as white as freshly fallen snow, blew out torrents of white-and-blue liquid crystal that solidified when they hit the air. The wall began to form, long and high but not strong enough to keep the demons, with their sharp claws, razor wings, and elongated fangs, from slicing through.

There simply wasn't time for the two ice dragons to build an impenetrable barrier.

The first set of demons broke through, crashing into the weakest and lowest part of the wall.

"Strengthen the barricade but fly backward."

The border guards did as commanded. Nut would not leave these dragons behind as they covered the caravan's retreat. No more sacrificed dragons.

The sky dragon hovered in the air, her eyes cast upward and to the stars above. She called to them, sparkling lights of order to the demons' chaos.

With a roared command, the stars above the demons lowered, and the sky below rose. The heavenly bodies stretched and arched, resembling a dragon on its back clawed feet while extending the massive girth of its body over a copse of trees, with its clawed front feet on the other side.

"I hold your souls between my sky," her voice boomed. *"You will not see the light of another day."*

Sky and stars corralled the demons, as the ice dragons not only built an ice wall but an ice fortress that encircled the demons.

The sky above the wall lifted, and the stars multiplied, creating a dome of cosmic energy.

"Go through the gateway," she ordered the ice dragons.

Taking off, Nut waited until the two dragons were safely through. She flew backward, her eyes on the prison and listening to the sound of demon claws scratching at the thick ice, followed by the thudding of rammed bodies against the prison.

When she reached the Gateway of the Two Ladies, a king cobra image of Wadjet on the right and Nekhbet, in vulture form, on the left of the arc, Nut took one last look at her beloved Nebty. For over a thousand years, dragons served as the gatekeepers, determining the preternaturals who would be permitted to leave their realm and travel to the realm of humans.

The goddesses created dragons for this very purpose, placing the floating island nation of Nebty, the name ancient Egyptians gave to the twin deities, in front of the gateway. No preternatural could pass through without permission from the King and Queen of Nebty—Geb and Nut.

Now, with the harsh sound of battle and the scent of blood carried on the wind, Nut's heart broke. Dragons were meant to protect the human realm at all cost. The Demon Kingdom could not be allowed to win, even if Geb and Nebty fell to King Sansabonsom.

Resolve had Nut flying through the gateway. Darkness and godly magic met her. From there, she could see both realms. The bright light of early morning in front of her and the dark clouds of midnight behind. The tunnel between the realms had many names, depending on the preternatural culture. Gargoyles called it Borlun, elves Gweyr, griffins Ghostcrest. For dragons, the tunnel was known as the Eye of Ra because it saw all.

Flying to the edge of the tunnel and cursing the traitorous dragons and opportunistic demons, Nut filled her belly with sky magic, breathed deep and brought it from her stomach, up her body and out her throat in a devastating rush of fire.

She scorched the Gateway of the Two Ladies and the Eye of Ra, refilling her lungs with fire and releasing it over and again until the gateway collapsed and the space between the realms disintegrated under the heat of her dragon fire.

Geb, forgive me.

—————◦—————

THE STORY CONTINUES...

ABOUT N.D. JONES

N. D. Jones is a USA Today Best-selling author. She lives in Maryland with her husband and two children. N.D. writes what she sees as a dearth in the romance genre--African/African American love with a paranormal twist. She spends a lot of time developing the mythology of her novels, as well as the execution of the paranormal element. When she writes a book with witches and shapeshifters, for example, she thinks it's important to show what it means to be a witch and shapeshifter. That's one thing a reader of books by N.D. can look forward to. The paranormal is not a sidebar in her novels. It's center stage and critical to the plot.

OTHER BOOKS BY N.D. JONES

Winged Warriors Novella Series (Angels and Demons)
Fire, Fury, Faith (Book 1)
Heat, Hunt, Hope (Book 2)

Death and Destiny Trilogy (Witches and Were-Cat Shifters)
Of Fear and Faith (Book 1)
Of Beasts and Bonds (Book 2)
Of Deception and Divinity (Book 3)

Forever Yours Series (Fantasy Romance)
Bound Souls (Book 1)

For N.D.'s latest releases, giveaways, and news, visit her at ndjonesparanormalpleasure.com.

You can also join the author's newsletter at https://www.ndjonespara-normalpleasure.com/newsletter/

CPSIA information can be obtained
at www.ICGtesting.com
Printed in the USA
LVHW11s2322171018
593993LV00001B/173/P